Dangerous Desires

J J Duke

Delta

First published in 1995
by HEADLINE BOOK PUBLISHING

10 9 8 7 6 5 4 3

ISBN 0 7472 5093 6

Typeset by Avon Dataset Ltd., Bidford-on-Avon, B50 4JH

Printed and bound in Great Britain by
Mackays of Chatham plc, Chatham, Kent

HEADLINE BOOK PUBLISHING
A division of Hodder Headline
338 Euston Road,
London NW1 3BH

www.headline.co.uk
www.hodderheadline.com

Dangerous
Desires

Chapter One

'I suppose you're used to this.'

'Used to what?'

'Used to women throwing themselves at you.'

'Is that what you did?'

'You know it is.'

'I thought we came to a mutual understanding that this would be a good idea. Have you changed your mind?'

'No . . .' It was just that now she was in his bedroom, sitting on the edge of his bed, she wondered how many other women had come to the same mutual understanding. She didn't voice that thought however.

John Sewell was dark, his naturally olive-coloured skin bronzed by the sun, his face craggy and strong-boned, his cheeks rather gaunt, his nose straight and symmetrical, his chin solid and square. His thick wavy black hair fell constantly, like a comma, over his forehead, occasionally brushing his bushy eyebrows. His eyes, the darkest feature of all, were what most women saw first: great pools of liquid mahogany, a bottomless pit of emotion, of knowledge and feeling where a woman could drown, go down forever, lost in the intensity of their unblinking gaze.

He was tall and strong, moving with the relaxed ease of someone whose physical strength was effortless.

1

Without the slightest embarrassment, despite the fact that she was still fully dressed, he unbuttoned his shirt and pulled it out of his trousers. His broad chest was covered in a thick mat of black hair, his arms shaped by hard, well-defined muscles. His belly was flat with deep hollows on either side carved by the tightness of his abdominal muscles. The muscles of his chest were so well defined that it looked like a hardened leather cuirass worn by a Roman centurion in some Hollywood epic.

As soon as he had stripped off his shirt he unzipped his faded blue jeans and pulled them down together with his white cotton boxer shorts. He had already kicked off his shoes and wasn't wearing any socks. His long legs were as powerful as his torso, hard fibrous tissue. His cock was slightly aroused, thrusting out of his curly black pubic hairs, its circumcised tip notably smoother than the rest of its length. His balls were large, the sac of his scrotum comparatively hairless.

He walked over to the bed and stood in front of her, still showing no embarrassment that he was naked and she was fully clothed. He touched his cheek with the back of his hand then ran a finger over her lips as though touching some precious piece of porcelain.

'And now you,' he said with a note of challenge in his voice.

As she stood up he stripped the counterpane off the bed, propped the pillows against the wall and arranged himself against them, his feet up and his ankles crossed. His dark brown eyes were watching her intently and he was smiling. She couldn't tell whether it was a smug smile.

Nadine was wearing her working clothes: a tight-fitting black skirt and a simple white silk blouse. She unbuttoned the blouse at the front and unzipped the skirt at the side. It was too tight to fall to the floor of its own accord. She had to wriggle out of it. She held her emotions in check trying to keep her mind in neutral. She didn't do this kind of thing. As far as she could remember, even bearing in mind that memory was a notoriously unreliable guide in such matters, she had never gone to bed with a man only hours after she'd met him.

She stepped out of the skirt and picked it up from the floor acutely aware of his eyes following every movement of her body. She folded the skirt over a small armchair, turning her back on him, conscious of the fact that he would be able to see her bottom and of the way the white teddy she was wearing dug deeply into the cleft between her buttocks as it dipped between her legs. She thanked some god somewhere that she was wearing decent lingerie, as she stripped her blouse over her shoulders and hung it, too, over the chair.

She had a good body. She was proud of it. She worked on it, exercised regularly and watched her diet with great care. She didn't mind him looking at her with those dark hooded eyes, shaded by the depth of his brow. She wanted him to look.

'Is this what you usually do?' she asked for no reason she could think of. She suddenly realised she did not want to hear the answer.

'This what?'

'Watch.'

'You're a beautiful woman.' He said it as if she were an inanimate object and for some reason she found that exciting. As his eyes roamed her body, confirming what he said, it was as if she could feel them brushing her flesh. She could not suppress a shudder.

Very deliberately she peeled the thin white shoulder straps of the teddy down over her arms. It had lacy cups that clung to her breasts but gave them little support. They did not need it. They were firm and very round, jutting out firmly from her chest. As the lace fell away her breasts were exposed. She looked down at them. Her nipples were hard, corrugated; her areolae, circles of tan brown, were prickled with tiny extrusions like pimples, born of her excitement. However she tried to control it, her body betrayed her.

She pulled the teddy down. Down over her slim, waspish waist, down over the flare of her hips, down until its crotch was inverted, clinging to the plane of her sex as though reluctant to break the intimate contact with her body. With a tug she freed it and the silky white material floated to her feet.

Her tights were translucent and grey, shiny and unladdered. They did not hide the sparsely haired triangle of her sex. The fine blond hairs – he could have guessed she'd be a natural blonde – were so neat they looked as though they had been combed to a point – a point that led to the junction of her thighs, like an arrow on the map of her body. She hooked

4

her fingers into the waistband of the tights.

'No,' he said.

'No?'

'I like them. Leave them on.'

'Isn't that a little impractical?' she asked.

'Do it.' He did not say 'please'.

She sat on the edge of the bed again and ran her fingers through her short blond hair, feeling it spring back into place. Her display had swollen his penis. It stood up straight, projecting from the top of his thighs at right angles. It was big, broad and long, the bulb of its glans like a giant acorn atop a shaft that was veined and coarse.

As she looked she saw it throb, engorging more. She felt her sex throb too. She was barely in control now. She had succeeded in keeping her mind blank, in pushing reason and good sense aside, but she could no longer control her excitement. She wanted this man and she wanted him now. She wanted to feel his hard, muscled body embracing her, wanted those strong arms wrapped around her, crushing her. She wanted that big throbbing cock filling her to the limit.

She turned and ran her hand up his thighs to brush his balls. She wanted to take the initiative. His cock pulsed at the touch. She slid her hand down his thigh, caressing it with the lightest of touches. Another twitch from his cock.

'Do you want me to suck it?' she asked, her voice betraying her passion, wavering and unmodulated.

'Yes,' he said simply. There was no 'if you don't mind' or 'I'd really love that'.

She knelt up on the bed, the nylon rasping against

her legs. Perhaps that's why he hadn't wanted her to take the tights off, perhaps he had no intention of fucking her. Maybe he was just going to lay there and expect her to take him in her mouth.

Fluid had escaped at the tip of his urethra, oozing out until it was the shape of a perfect tear, viscous and sticky. Nadine touched it with the very tip of her tongue, pulling back so the string of liquid was spun out, like a spider's web, connecting her lips and his cock. The string finally broke. She dipped again and repeated the process. This time when the connection snapped she plunged her head down on to his hard erect shaft, right the way down until his cock was buried inside her mouth. She closed her lips around its base and felt the curls of his pubic hair against her chin.

Her body churned. His cock was big and hot and hard, hard like a bone, harder than she remembered any man before. She sucked on it, sucking without moving her mouth, feeling her sex throb as she imagined – not consciously but reflexively – how it would feel pressed deep inside her. Reflexively too she flexed her thighs, squeezing her labia together as she did when she was alone, in the prelude to masturbation. She could feel the sap of her body spreading out from her loins.

She slid her lips to the top of his penis and began a rhythmic motion. He moaned slightly. She did not allow his cock to come all the way out, just to the gate of her lips where her tongue flicked at the tiny slit of his urethra. Then she plunged down again, all the way, so that his glans nudged right up to the back of her throat. Then she pushed harder, controlling her gagging reflex as she had learned to do with other lovers, and felt his cock jam hard against the ribbed wall of her windpipe. At the same time she fingered his balls, jiggling them against her chin as though her fingers were practising their dexterity.

'No,' he said suddenly his hands gripping her head and pulling her mouth away.

'I don't mind.'

'That's not what I want. I want you. I need to fuck you.' The word 'fuck' sounded different on his lips. It sounded as if it were something she had never done before.

He was pulling her down on to her back while he rose to his knees. As soon as she was settled he leant forward and kissed her lightly on the lips, his mouth just brushing hers, moving from one side to the other, his tongue darting out in little forays to penetrate fleetingly into her moist clinging mouth. It was teasing, playful, increasing her need. She moaned, wanting more, arching up off the bed by way of a plea. But he paid no attention. He moved his mouth to her neck, sucking and licking and nibbling at her flesh, making her arch her head back in ecstasy against the sheets.

She felt her whole body being stretched, the teasing kisses like the ratchet on a medieval rack, pulling her body out until every tendon was taut. His mouth followed the graceful curve of her neck down to the hollows of her throat, over her collarbone, to the rise of her breasts. And while his mouth descended, the fingertips of his hand caressed her belly, drawing imaginary circles with the faintest of touches.

Nadine was stretched out like an elastic band, her whole body quivering, as his mouth approached her nipple. She could hardly wait for his lips to encircle the swollen, erect cherry that topped her breast. It seemed to be alive, wanting of its own accord, independent of the need Nadine felt, the need he had so artfully created. Suddenly she felt his hot breath blowing on her puckered flesh. Her nipple hardened further despite the fact it was already as hard as a pebble. Slowly, with infinite patience, she felt his tongue, hot and wet, stretch out to lick the very tip of her nipple, touching it so softly and with such tenderness that her response was emotional as well as sexual. He made her feel that he cared, he made her feel that he wanted to touch her with his mind as well as with his body.

His tongue circled the little button of flesh, barely making contact and yet evoking ripples of pleasure in her body that tightened the rack she was laid on to breaking point.

He moved his mouth down the slope of her breast and across to the other pillow of flesh, little kisses, like footsteps, marking the way. When he reached the top of the rise, his tongue flicked out again, the touch of a butterfly on the stamen of her breast.

At the same time, with the same gentleness, she felt his hand running down under her tights and his finger insinuating itself between her legs. She opened them wider, allowing him in, opening the gates to her body, her labia parting to reveal the little promontory of her clitoris. It was throbbing. His finger nudged against it with the touch of a feather and a delicacy that perfectly matched her needs.

The feelings from the three cardinal points on her body joined together, the impression he had left on one nipple almost as strong as the actual feeling from the other. In a subtle, sinuous motion the movement of his tongue, circular and slow, synchronised with the movement of his finger.

She knew she was coming, coming on sensations so delicate she would never have believed it possible, but coming hard and hot. The ripples he had created built into crested waves that threw her down on the shore of their passion, down into a pit of exquisite sensation. The intensity and the suddenness took her by surprise, and she gasped, a long low animal noise rattling in her throat.

She tried to sit up. She wanted to put her arms around him, to pull him down on her to express her need for him, the need that her orgasm had only intensified. She wanted to feel that bone-hard cock plunging into the dark passage of her sex, to feel it filling her, overwhelming her, to feel her body closing around it and making it hers. But he resisted, pushing her back onto the sheet.

'Please . . .'

'Be patient,' he said like an adult talking to a child. He made her feel like a child eager for knowledge. He made her feel as though she had never had sex before.

Extracting his hand from her tights he ran both

hands over her nylon-covered belly. The skin on his palms was rough, like a workman's hands, and she could hear it rasping against the nylon of her tights until it reached the apex of her thighs. The seam of the tights bisected her belly, following the furrow of her sex. With his thumb and forefinger he picked up the tuck of the seam and then, with an ease that belied the effort it must have required, tore a long hole in the nylon. In seconds he had enlarged it so the whole of her sex was exposed.

'That's better.' He was admiring his work, staring down into her lap as if appreciating some complex art form.

His finger slid into the crease of her labia. She felt her sticky juices against it. As he registered it too, he looked into her eyes and she was drowning again, just as she had when he'd first walked through her office door no more than four hours earlier. At the time she had thought she had never felt such raw physical attraction for any man, totally uncluttered by social niceties. Now that attraction was translated into reality and she knew her instincts had been right. She had never responded sexually like this before, never come as effortlessly, or with such intensity. It was as if he'd found a switch to her sexuality and simply flicked it on.

She opened her legs, spreading them apart, and watched his eyes examine the fully exposed delta of her sex. The fleece of her pubis did not extend between her thighs. Her labia were hairless, thin, neat and unusually smooth, they made a perfect elongated oval.

His finger found her clitoris and she abandoned conscious thought, her sex demanding all her attention. The residue of her orgasm lingered in the little nodule of nerves, sensitising it, tenderising it, so that his first touch felt like an electric shock. She moaned. It sounded like a moan of pain. His finger was hardly touching her, it was like the touch of the softest feather, but he knew it was more than enough to provoke her.

Sewell rocked back on his haunches watching her. The only contact between their bodies was his finger-tip brushing against her clitoris with deliberate delicacy. As he moved the tip against the tiny promontory, he saw her body arch off the bed and knew she was coming again. The great gash he had torn in her tights excited him. Her sex was so open and vulnerable in contrast to the tight nylon that sheathed her thighs. It was a contrast of textures, the nylon shiny and coarse, the flesh smooth and creamy.

Nadine could hardly stand it. Feelings so sharp they were almost painful, flooded through her. His touch was perfect – the perfect pressure, the perfect motion. At first she had closed her eyes but now she forced them open to look up at him. His mouth was smiling that cruel, knowing smile. She looked down at his single finger moving almost imperceptibly between her legs as it rolled over and around and up her clitoris. But she couldn't look for long. She felt the circle of orgasm closing rapidly and, as her body shuddered her eyes were forced shut and light exploded in her head, every nerve and muscle quivering as another climax broke over her.

11

Before she knew what was happening he had fallen on her like a wolf on its prey, burying his cock so deeply inside her it took her breath away. She could hardly breath at all. She was existing on sensation, the purest sensation she had ever experienced.

She came again immediately, the second his cock hit the neck of her womb, her whole sex contracting around his big, rock-hard shaft, squeezing it, milking it. Her orgasm gained its own momentum, exploding higher and longer than she'd ever thought possible. He moved inside her without subtlety or finesse, using all his considerable power to pump into her. Nadine did not know whether she was having one continuous orgasm, or several joined together so closely she could not tell where one began and the other ended.

She felt his body tense as he drove himself up into her as far as he could go and she thought she could not come again. But then she felt another sensation she had never experienced before, whether imaginary or real she could not tell. The top of her vagina seemed to swell, as though he had opened the door to a secret garden. She felt his cock pulse and then begin to spasm. In her mind's eyes she could see it, his semen spurting into the secret place he had discovered.

They were shaking, quivering together, clinging to each other as if their lives depended on it.

Eventually it must have stopped, but she could not move, or speak. She could barely register thought. She knew one thing. She had never felt like this in her life before.

* * *

Nadine had arranged to meet him in her office. She didn't like the ritual of business lunches; two hours of small talk followed by fifteen minutes of business to justify the expense. If he wasn't inclined to accept her suggestion, steak tartare and Burgundy wasn't going to change his mind.

Up to that point she knew him only by reputation and his reputation was intimidating. The best graphic artist in the business bar none, he was known to be difficult; a man with a sharp tongue who did not suffer fools gladly. She had been advised to avoid him but she wanted the best. The best graphics for the product was the only way she was going to get the new account for her advertising agency. And it was an account she wanted badly. The Brandling Corporation were big spenders, their billings totalling more than any of the agency's existing clients. There were three new products to launch, involving a huge television spend as well as newspaper and magazine advertising. If she could get that for her company they would have no option but to make her a director. And that was definitely her next goal.

He was fifteen minutes late but did not apologise.

Nadine would never forget the first impact of seeing him as her secretary showed him into her office. It was a physical impact, like a slap in the face. He was simply the most attractive man she could imagine. She liked to think of herself as a modern and independent woman, but this took her by surprise, a throwback to girlhood when men had been objects of fantasy fulfilment. It was minutes – or so it seemed – before she realised she was staring, her mouth open.

John Sewell made no comment. He was used to the effect he had on women. He was used to the stares, the stuttering responses, the weak handshakes and embarrassed blushes. Used to it and capable, if it suited him, of using it.

'Mr Sewell, I'm Nadine Davies,' she said, trying to sound businesslike. She stood up and extended her hand.

'John please, Mr Sewell makes me sound like my father.' He shook her hand firmly and she felt his hard callused skin, like ageing leather.

'John then. Can we get you tea or coffee?' Her secretary, obviously equally taken with the man, hovered behind him, waiting for instructions.

'Nothing, thank you.'

'Thank you, Dawn,' Nadine said noting how disappointed the girl looked as she backed out of the office. 'Please . . .' Nadine indicated the chair in front of her desk, trying not to see the way he looked at her, his mahogany eyes boring into her and through her.

He was wearing grey corduroy trousers, a dark blue denim shirt and a red cashmere V-necked sweater, with short brown leather boots. He seemed to glide into the chair curling his big body into it and crossing his legs, his fingers interlaced on his lap. His dark eyes looked up again. This time she could not avoid his gaze. As he studied her with interest she felt as though her whole life was laid out in front of him, her needs, desires, ambitions – and weaknesses.

'So what can I do for you, Ms Davies?' He stressed the 'Ms', an essential credential for a New Man. His voice was like velvet.

'Nadine,' she said.

'So, Nadine?'

'Well . . .' She tried to concentrate. It wasn't easy. What she actually wanted to do was ask him if he'd mind taking her straight to the nearest convenient bed. '. . . you've heard of the Brandling Corporation. We're pitching for their account. They are launching three new products and they want to start with a new image across the whole range. They want a corporate logo that suggests quality, value for money, home-town values, that sort of thing. Obviously, in my view, the graphics are the key to it. I think some of our rivals will be pitching with a smart television commercial but I think Brandling will respect a more, shall we say, old-fashioned approach.'

'Is that all?'

'All?' She didn't understand that response.

'You could have called my agents. They'd have organised it. . .'

'I wanted to meet you personally.'

'And why was that?' he said sharply, suspecting the answer. His body language was as fluent as his movement, relaxed and confident. He did not use his hands to emphasise his speech.

'Because . . .' She struggled to find the words. His directness had caught her out.

'Because you want me to work for nothing?' he suggested.

'No, no of course not. It's just the politics here. Brandling turned the agency down last year and my boss doesn't think it's worth spending any money to try again.'

'Why should I care whether you succeed or not?'

At that moment Nadine could not think of a single reason. All the carefully prepared arguments she had rehearsed had drifted away from her in the cross currents of his mahogany eyes.

'I can't think of a reason,' she said truthfully.

'Then I'm wasting my time,' he said but made no effort to get up.

'I need this account. It's important to me,' she said falteringly.

'But not to me.'

'You're the best.'

'That's why I get paid a great deal of money.'

'I can give you five hundred pounds out of my own pocket.' Up until now she had never considered doing any such thing.

'You're a very attractive woman, Ms Davies,' he said, reverting to the more formal title. He had been looking out of the window but turned to flash his eyes at her again. It was like being hit by a bolt of lightning. She was glad she was sitting down. 'Did you think I'd work for nothing because of the way you looked? That I'd be seduced by your feminine charm?'

'No, no, of course not.' Nadine felt a flush of anger at the suggestion. It was an anger based on guilt for she frequently used her looks to get men to do what she wanted.

'What then?'

'I thought . . . developing a new image for the Brandling Corporation would be a fascinating challenge.'

'Nothing in this business challenges me, Ms Davies. I am an artist. A struggling artist. I use the money I earn from all the crap to fund my early retirement.'

'Retirement?'

'Yes, so I can stop designing packets of soap flakes and do what I want to do.'

'Be a real artist?' She could not keep a hint of mockery out of her voice.

'Exactly.'

'I thought artists were meant to be starving?' she said sarcastically. 'Doesn't poverty enhance the creative spirit?'

'You're full of shit,' he said with no emotion.

'Well, doesn't it?' She felt her hackles rise. She hated people who despised the world of commerce, who were happy to take its money but looked down on it from the heights of intellectual or artistic superiority.

'If you want me to take that question seriously, no it doesn't. Do you really believe it is necessary to have no money, to live in squalor, to produce real art?'

'No. But neither do I believe it is necessary to bite the hand that feeds you.'

'You're proud of all this then, are you? Selling things to people that they don't need.'

'It's provided you with a very good living, I see.'

She looked at the Rolex on his wrist and the cashmere sweater.

'Why shouldn't I get top dollar?'

'From all those people you despise?' She spat the words out, unable to help herself, her face flushed with emotion. His face, calm, with a smug complacent smile that suggested she couldn't possibly understand what he was talking about, annoyed her even more.

He looked at her steadily, studying her.

'OK,' he said simply.

'OK what?' she said, the anger still in her voice.

'OK, I'll do it for five hundred pounds. On one condition.' He was still smiling but no longer smugly. His smile was warm and open and forgiving, a smile that included her in his world, a smile that made her feel special.

'And what's that?'

'It's five now. What time do you finish?'

'Six.'

'I'll wait.'

'What's the condition?'

'That you take me out and buy me a bottle of champagne. Vintage champagne. Louis Roederer Cristal preferably.'

Nadine felt her anger melt like snow in the full sunlight of his eyes. His expression seemed no longer to be condescending but to envelop her, implying a conspiracy that only the two of them knew and understood the real world and how it worked.

'Done,' she said, wanting to ask him why he had changed his mind so quickly but deciding not to.

And that was how it had started. Four hours later they were in bed together.

'You're not asleep?'

'How can you tell?'

'Your breathing's too shallow and your body's too still.'

'I was trying not to wake you.'

The bedroom curtains were drawn but the grey light of dawn still filtered through.

Nadine was lying on her side, Sewell on his back, the pliant flesh of her buttocks just touching the side of his thigh.

'It's still early.' For some reason she was whispering.

'Have you slept at all?'

'A little.'

'Will you sleep more?'

'I don't usually do this sort of thing,' she said.

'What sort of thing?'

'Going to bed with men I've only just met.'

'Don't you? You surprise me,' he said in a mocking tone.

'You, I suppose, are used to women throwing themselves at you.'

'I thought we'd agreed. We came to a mutual agreement over a bottle of very good champagne that it would be mutually beneficial if we continued our liaison in my bed.'

'We did. You didn't answer my question.'

'What question?'

'Are you used to women throwing themselves at you?'

'It wasn't a question,' he interrupted. 'It was a statement.'

'So now it's a question. Are you?'

'Yes, I am,' he said simply. 'And you are no doubt used to men flinging themselves at your feet.'

'That's entirely different. That's biological programming. Men will go after women automatically. It's a reflex for a man to make a pass at a woman. It's like breathing – as long as they're alive, they do it.'

'And women don't?'

'You know they don't.'

He turned on his side, spooning his body against hers and wrapping his arms around her, one arm under her neck, one over her body. She felt his flaccid cock trapped between her buttocks and his stomach. His hands cupped her breasts, squeezing them gently while his mouth kissed the back of her neck. She felt goose bumps spring up on her arm. He kissed the bones at the top of her spine and her shoulder blades. Almost instantly his cock began to unfurl.

'You're so soft,' he whispered in her ear. 'Would the idea of my coming inside you again be acceptable?'

'You think I've changed my mind?'

'No, I just don't want to appear greedy.'

'Be greedy,' she said and meant it, a wave of excitement rushing through her, the idea of having his hard, strong and large cock inside her again, making her sex throb. She wriggled her bottom against him and his penis, growing rapidly, buried itself in the deep cleft of her fleshy arse.

He moved his hands so he could hold her nipples, rolling them between his fingers and thumbs.

'You're making me hard,' he said, stating the obvious.

'Good. I want you hard.' She could feel his phallus was fully erect now, bedded comfortably between the thick pillows of her buttocks. It pulsed and throbbed, like a small animal with a life of its own.

He moved away from her, angling his cock down until it nudged against the puckered crater of her anus. It was deliberate, he knew he was not pushing into her sex.

'No,' she said at once, a frisson of fear making her goose bumps return.

'No what?' he said innocently, his cock in the same position and pushing forward slightly.

'I'm not ready for that.'

'For what?'

'I don't want you to bugger me, Sewell.'

'Don't you like it?'

'I don't know.'

'I see.' He bucked his hips and his cock slid into the furrow of her labia and she was astonished at how wet she was. 'So you've never . . .' he found the opening of her vagina '. . . done it . . .' He pushed forward slightly allowing her sex to anoint him with her juices. '. . . you've never had . . .' He plunged forward, riding up into her without the slightest difficulty, her juices so copious she could hardly believe it, or was it the residue of his earlier spending? '. . . a man's cock in your arse?'

'No,' she gasped as she felt his cock sliding into

her again, overwhelming her with its power. She had lied to him. She had attempted it once but it had been too painful. Perhaps, with the right man, she might try again, but it was not what she wanted from Sewell now. What she wanted was what she was getting, his hard, strong cock pounding into her sex, filling it completely. She used all her internal muscles to squeeze it, wanting to feel its extraordinary hardness. She gripped it tight, reading its contours like a blindman reads braille. It was just as hard as it had been last night.

Her vagina was sore. It had taken a hammering. But it was a soreness that made her more sensitive, that accelerated her excitement.

One of his hands left her breast. It snaked down over her belly and infiltrated between her thighs. In seconds she felt a finger stroke her clitoris. As he began to power his cock in and out of her, he moved her clitoris up and down with his finger, pressing it against the bone underneath.

This double attack on her senses made her reel.

'Is this what you want?' he taunted through clenched teeth.

'Yes,' she managed to hiss.

'Like this?' he said as he bucked forward.

'Yes, yes . . .'

A few minutes before Nadine had been at rest, lying quietly in a stranger's bed. Now her body was seething with desire. He seemed to know instinctively what to do to please her sexually, things she herself didn't even know she liked. But her intense excitement wasn't just physical. There was something about what he was, something about his manner, something about him that turned her on. It was the situation too, the fact that she had abandoned all her age-old taboos, all the shibboleths she had cherished for so long. She had let herself go, jumped without a safety net. That thrilled her.

She shook her head from side to side as if trying to clear her thoughts, to decide what she wanted. She wanted to take the initiative.

'Wait,' she said pulling away from him. She wriggled around and came up onto her knees. She stripped aside the bedding and looked down at his body in the grey early morning light as he rolled onto his back. His cock stuck up from his loins, glistening as if it had been dipped in oil.

'No?' He looked at her quizzically. 'I thought it felt good.'

'It did but now I want this . . .' She swung her thigh over her hips. The tip of his penis nudged between her thighs.

'Why?'

'Because I want to see you,' she said. It was partially true. She also, for once, wanted to be in control. Reaching behind her back she took his cock in her hand and guided it between her labia.

His dark brown eyes were looking at her with amusement. He laced his fingers together behind his head, the muscles at the side of his ribs and his abdomen clearly defined like the rungs of a ladder. He was beautiful. Everything about him spoke of strength and power and masculinity.

Still holding his erection, Nadine sunk down

slightly on her haunches, feeling his glans nose up into her body, the mouth of her vagina closing around it as if in a kiss.

'I want you,' she said unnecessarily.

'Take me then,' he mocked.

And she did. She dropped herself onto his cock and felt it stabbing up into her, much deeper than it had been minutes before. The silky velvety flesh of her sex closed around it, a custom-made sheath for the knife of his phallus.

He began to buck his hips under her, his strength lifting her body, as he thrust up into her.

'Will you come for me?' he said.

'Yes, oh yes . . .'

'I want to see it.'

'Watch then.' She would come easily. She had what she wanted now. She feasted her eyes on him. She had wanted to possess him, to have him, for him to be hers. It was an illusion, of course, at any moment he could have thrown her down on the bed and possessed *her*. But the illusion was enough. As he pumped into her, she in turn rode him, his pelvis beneath her like a saddle. She allowed herself to be lifted by him then she dropped all her weight on him as he fell back on the bed, plunging his cock deeper, right up against the neck of her womb.

Her breasts were flying up and down so violently she had to catch them in her hands. As she cupped them she felt them respond. She squeezed them hard, pinching her nipples, and felt a jolt of pleasure stab through her.

Nadine looked down at Sewell. Even through the

blur of motion she could see he wasn't looking at her body, so wantonly displayed, but straight into her eyes. He looked at her as though it was her blue irises that were the centre of her sex, the most sensitive points in her body that needed to be touched by his stare. And he was right.

Her orgasm was sudden, not unexpected but surprising nonetheless. One moment she was in control, her body able to cope with the rush of feelings that assailed it, her mind weaving images of sex, images of the night before, images of Sewell, into a tapestry of emotion to hang in her memory. The next moment she felt her body and mind gripped by a paroxysm of raw sensation that locked every muscle and jammed every nerve.

She managed to force herself down on him so his erection was buried in the depths of her, but she could do nothing more, only feel.

Sensing her crisis, Sewell stopped too, using his strength to arch up into her and hold himself there, knowing she needed nothing more.

'God,' she said quietly as she tried to keep her eyes open to look into those dark brown pools of light that gazed at her so knowingly but she lost the battle. As the force of orgasm screwed her eyes shut, she could still see him on the backdrop of her mind, his eyes boring into her soul.

Eventually the crisis passed. The rigidity of her body disappeared and she could open her eyes again. He was smiling slightly, his hands still laced behind his head, an infuriating self-satisfaction in his manner which reflected the ease with which he had been able to make her come.

'What about you?' As if to illustrate her point she squeezed his cock with the muscles of her vagina. She wished she hadn't. Her body was seized with a tremor, echoes of her orgasm like the aftershock of an earthquake that shook every nerve.

'I was waiting for you,' he said. He removed his hands from behind his head and stroked her arms gently. 'There's so many things I want to do with you, so many ways I want to please you.'

'I want to please you too, Sewell,' she said firmly. There was something about him that made her feel like a child. She usually resented men who made her feel this way, but it was not resentment she felt for him. It was quite a different emotion.

He was looking at her steadily, his eyes full of lust. He gripped her arms firmly and pulled her over to the side and onto her back, his erection slipping out of her body. He moved round so he could kiss her, his lips hard against hers, his tongue plunging into her mouth as hot as his cock had been.

She felt his wet erection against her hip.

'What do you want me to do?' she asked.

'You're doing it.'

He rolled on top of her. The missionary position. She wanted to mock him, taunt him for not wanting her to be on top. Was he old-fashioned? Did he have to be in control? Didn't he know the New Man was supposed to be able to accept subordination? But somehow none of these questions were relevant to him. What is more, she wanted it like this, she wanted to be crushed underneath him, to feel that strong, hard body on top of her again.

But that was not what he had in mind apparently, not yet anyway. His hands were rolling her over onto her stomach and almost before she knew what was happening he had drawn her up to her knees, his hands pulling her hips. He knelt behind her.

She opened her legs. She feared he was going to try and bugger her again but, though his cock touched the bud of her anus, making her gasp, he quickly moved it up to her vagina, her wetness making the movement frictionless.

'You make me so hard,' he said. It was self-evidently true. He thrust forward and she felt his erection invading her again. Despite her recent orgasm her body reacted so intensely she knew instantly he was going to make her come again.

Nadine pulled herself up onto all fours. It changed the angle of his phallus inside her, allowing it to delve deeper. She looked up. It was quite light in the room now, the sun up, the shadows dispelled. She hadn't noticed it last night but on the wall opposite the foot of the bed was a rectangular mirror in a black frame. She was facing it. She could see the reflection of her body and Sewell kneeling behind her. His face was set, his eyes looking down at her body, at her long back and the ridge of her spine and at her round, soft, buttocks pressing against his belly. She could see his firm muscles, his hands gripping her by the hips, his biceps flexed and well-defined, the contours of his abdomen like a drawing in some anatomical textbook with each set of muscles clearly visible.

The image in the mirror fascinated Nadine. It was the perfect representation of what she felt. The whole night had been unreal and Sewell like some character from a film. She could not believe what she had done. Or what she was doing now, kneeling on all fours, being taken by a man she did not know, a stranger. They were two strangers making love. More accurately they were two strangers making lust, overwhelmed by a physical need that was greater than the social decencies.

She stared into the mirror and the strangers stared back.

Is that what had happened? Has lust got the better of her. She couldn't think. Her body was humming like a radio, the background noise and static beginning to recede as she found the right frequency and the signal became clearer and sharper.

Sewell was sliding his penis into her with great deliberation, each thrust a journey that seemed to last forever. She felt her vagina closing as his cock slipped out, and opening up again as it was forced back in. She could feel every contour of him, every vein delineated, the ridge around the glans a rib that moved sinuously inside her. She could feel his balls banging into her too, a pendulum that hit her on every swing.

She wanted to show him she knew what to do, that she was a woman, and experienced at that. Supporting herself with one arm she reached between her legs and groped to find his balls. She reeled them in with her fingers, his scrotum wet and slippery from her juices.

'Yes,' he said at once.

She squeezed the balls gently. He thrust forward and stopped. She squeezed again. She was milking him. He was deep inside her body, so deep she could have rubbed her navel and felt the outline of his erection. As she squeezed she felt his cock spasm. He was letting her make him come. What she was doing was enough. She squeezed and he jerked against the confines of her silky wet sex.

'Yes,' he repeated.

She pulled his balls down hard, pulling them down away from their bodies. She felt them pulsing in her hand and at the same time his cock jerked more violently too. He was out of control. He pulled out slightly then rammed himself back in, harder and deeper than he had been before, pulling her back onto him with all his strength, his hands pressed deep into the flesh of her hips.

She felt his ejaculation. His cock jerked wildly inside her. She felt the rush of wetness. Gently she squeezed his balls again, as if to extract every last drop.

His orgasm had provoked her. She felt her body changing gear. She'd accomplished her aim, showed him she was not naive, not a child of innocence to this man of experience. Now her body wanted its reward.

Looking up into the mirror she stared into his face. More than anything, more than his hard pulsing cock, or his strong muscled body, or the incredible feeling of wetness that oozed out of her, it was the look on his face, an expression of abandon and ecstasy, that catapulted her into orgasm.

His cock was still erect. With the last of her energy she pushed back on it and felt it nosing up into her again, back against all the nerves that had been so sorely used. It was the last straw. Her orgasm seized her, shuddering through her, the sensation radiating out from her sex like the ripples on a pond disturbed by a stone. The physical sensation was transmuted into emotion. She fought to keep her eyes open, wanting to see the expression on her face, wanting to see her own ecstasy but her eyelids fell and her mind was filled with a chiaroscuro of crimson and scarlet and flickering shadows.

Chapter Two

When she woke up again they were lying side by side, their bodies covered by a single sheet, his breathing heavy and regular. Nadine had been woken by an urgent need to pee.

Trying not to disturb him, she pulled the sheet aside and slipped out of bed. She had no idea where the bathroom was. Last night they had gone straight to the bedroom and stayed there. She looked around. Her white teddy was on the floor where it had fallen, her torn and ruined tights at the side of the bed where they'd finally been discarded after their first session.

The bedroom was surprisingly neat. Nadine might have expected Sewell's house to be chaotic but it was orderly and uncluttered. It was furnished in a combination of modern and antique furniture that blended perfectly together. The bedroom was a symphony of creams, beige and oatmeal, clearly decorated with an artist's eye for colour, the walls magnolia, the carpet off-white, the counterpane — now lying on the floor at the foot of the bed – a rough-textured oatmeal. There was a large modern chest of drawers made from satinwood with each drawer outlined in a lemon wood marquetry and a wardrobe in the same style. On the wall by the door was a snowscape so good it made Nadine feel cold despite the warmth in the room. Remembering their first bad-tempered conversation, she wondered if it were one of Sewell's.

The bedside tables were antique, as was the Victorian button-backed saloon chair where she had folded her skirt and blouse. There was no bric-a-brac on any of the surfaces and no alarm clock.

She walked as quietly as she could out into the hall. There were three doors, all in the same stripped pine finish. She opened the nearest and discovered a small compact bathroom tiled in square grey tiles. There was an attractive modern bathroom suite in white with dramatically sculpted lines and a shower screen around the bath.

Nadine sat on the toilet seat, looking around as she did so. The room was as neat as the bedroom, no clutter on the surfaces, no shampoo bottles, or Kleenex, or dental floss. There was a white soap bowl on one corner of the bath filled with cream-coloured soaps of different sizes and a big natural sponge. On a shelf above the washhand basin stood a small ceramic vase containing a disposable razor, a tube of toothpaste and three toothbrushes. A white towelling-robe hung from a stainless steel hook behind the door.

Nadine examined her naked body in the long mirror on the wall above the bath. Apart from tousled hair – which she combed with her fingers – her body betrayed no evidence of debauchery.

She wandered out into the hall. She should have gone back to bed but she could hear Sewell's regular breathing and allowed her curiosity to get the better of her. She wanted to see his paintings. After the passion he had displayed in her office she was more than interested to see whether his 'retirement' would be justified. If the snowscape in the bedroom was an example it probably was.

The second door in the hall opened on to what was obviously a spare room. There were a couple of prints on the wall but they were both signed and not Sewell's work. Behind the third door she discovered an uncarpeted wooden staircase. Hesitantly, like a child sneaking a look at Christmas presents before Christmas day, she tip-toed up the stairs. Halfway up, on a kite step that turned the stairs to the left, the boards creaked loudly under her weight. She almost got cold feet. But she stopped and listened and heard no movement and decided to carry on. So what if Sewell did wake to find her? She'd tell him the truth, that she wanted to see his work. He couldn't criticise her curiosity after what they had just been through together.

As she turned the second leg of the staircase she saw a bank of windows set into the roof, a large slanting skylight, no doubt pointing north. The studio ran the whole width of the house. The attic had been converted to provide an open space, with bare floorboards, unplastered brick walls and exposed rafters.

The room was full of big canvasses, mostly on their wooden stretchers and stacked three or four deep.

Even at the most cursory inspection she realised the snowscape downstairs was not painted by Sewell or, if it had been, represented a completely different phase of his work. The subject of all the pictures she could see, without riffling through the stacks, was quite the opposite of landscape. It was sex. And not just naked men and women but naked men and women highly *engagé*.

Picking her way across the oil-paint-stained floorboards, Nadine rounded the large easel that stood at the far end of the room. A canvas was mounted on it, though the picture looked more or less finished. Sewell had a striking style, the paint being applied thickly in vivid colours, but though his method was far from naturalistic it was surprising how much mood and emotion and physical presence the pictures exuded. The painting on the easel was a simple tableau. In the foreground, a short-haired brunette stood with her left hand resting against the top of a button-backed Victorian saloon chair like the one in the bedroom below. She was naked apart from black high-heeled shoes, the lines of her body outlined in thick white brush strokes. She was not tall but had an hour-glass figure, her narrow waist in contrast to her big, pendulant breasts and rich generous hips. The hair of her pubis was thick and bushy, an irregular triangle of swirling black paint.

Kneeling on the floor in front of her was another woman, also naked but this time with no shoes. She had short hair too but hers was blond, the paint the colour of golden corn in bright sunlight. She was seen in profile, her breasts firm and round, but not as large as the brunette's, an equally round bottom resting on her trim heels.

The two women were looking at each other and it was obvious that something had happened between them, something sexual and something that had been, for whatever reason, interrupted. The emotional impact of the painting was extraordinary. Nadine could feel the women's excitement and their shock that something had gone wrong.

It was only when she stood back slightly from the canvas that she realised what it was. In the background the colours forming the walls of the room and a large double bed were shades of brown and blue. But to one side, Nadine could see an open doorway and in it the figure of a man. She could only make out his face, dark eyes and black hair, but the more she stared the more the situation became clear. He was gazing at the two women with shock certainly but with shock inextricably mixed with another emotion: lust. His expression seemed to change as she stared, the shock giving way to excitement. He had interrupted the women in some sexual intimacy but, far from being disgusted by it, he found their behaviour arousing. Or was that Nadine's reaction? Was she transferring her own feelings into the man's perspective and imposing her own scenario on the scene?

Whatever it was, the painting haunted her. It created another reaction too. Whatever the two women had been doing was so intimate and so profound that suddenly Nadine felt embarrassed to be party to it. She felt herself blushing.

Backing away from the canvas she went to the nearest stack of pictures. The first in the pile featured the same brunette. She knew it was the same woman despite the fact that the painting made no attempt at portraiture. The impression of the woman Sewell had created was as easily identifiable as any photographic portrait. The brunette had a personality Nadine could read as clearly as if it were written in a book. The man in this picture was the same man as the man in the first, though this time his dark brooding presence was in the foreground. The couple stood in what looked like a living room, the man naked but for a white shirt, standing in three-quarters profile, the tails of his shirt covering his buttocks but not his erection. The woman stood in front of him, her finger just about to touch the circumcised tip of his glans, her body naked as before, except for black high-heels.

Looking carefully, she saw a third figure, another woman sitting in an armchair in the background. She was fully dressed and not painted in any detail except for her eyes which expressed not excitement but weariness, as though she had seen it all before and didn't particularly care to see it again.

Nadine's reaction to this painting was the same as to the first. Her imagination ran riot. Not only did the man's cock seem to throb visibly but the inner thigh of the woman, where it was not covered with her extended growth of pubic hair, seemed to be wet, as though the flesh-coloured paint had not dried. Her nipples too, painted low on her pendulant breasts, seemed to fluoresce, suggesting her heat and excitement. The picture captured – or created – a moment in time expressing perfectly its implications and consequences.

Nadine would have liked to flick through all the paintings but dared not. She definitely did not want to be caught going through this collection. They were too private and too personal. If Sewell wanted to show her, and she hoped he would, that was fine, but his vision clearly had to be viewed by appointment only.

She headed for the stairs but, just as she was about to go down, her eye was caught by the first painting in a stack tucked away on the wall behind the banisters that surrounded the top of the staircase. Most of Sewell's paintings that she had seen were characterised by brooding shadows and dark colours, light being used to illuminate an area as a way of concentrating the attention. In contrast this painting was blinding.

It was not only the use of light that attracted her but the subject. As well as being set in the bedroom she had just left, the creamy colours of the walls and carpet making the picture so bright, it was a reproduction of what she had been doing and, from the way the light filtered through the gauzy curtains, the same time of day.

The short-haired brunette was kneeling on all fours on the bed, her back straight, her knees apart. The dark brooding man was behind her, his body pressed against her buttocks, his face, for the first time in all the paintings, distinct. It was Sewell. Though the brush strokes that made up his face were broad and thick there was no mistaking his personality, those brown knowing eyes, the sexual

37

magnetism, the sheer animal attraction. Nor, in the way his body was depicted was there any doubt about his power and potency.

The brunette had her head up almost at right angles to her spine. Just as Nadine had done, she was staring into the mirror where the scene on the bed was reflected in miniature.

There was one major difference from what Nadine had just experienced however. Kneeling on the bed alongside the man, was the short-haired blonde from the first picture. She had one hand on the brunette's buttock and the other disappeared down behind the man's back.

There was little doubt from the expression of the brunette's face and the rigidity of her body that she was experiencing an orgasm, in fact, that she was in the first throes of it. Sewell had captured the explosive energy perfectly, the moment the eyes light up with passion, surprised and delighted by the first rush of pleasure.

The blonde was excited too but she gave the impression of being satiated, as if her body could not take any more. She had summoned enough energy from somewhere to take part in this final tableau but her emotions were thoroughly exhausted.

As with all the other pictures Nadine was astonished how, with such thickly applied paint and relatively crude technique, Sewell had managed to conjure up so much emotion. She could feel what the brunette was feeling, the depth of penetration, and the strength of the orgasm that assailed her.

More than that, she could read the relationship between the three characters. There was a kind of love there but definitely no friendship. There was need, a strong mutual need, but no mutual respect. They were fucking, not making love. Nadine had the feeling that the blonde resented what the man had made her feel.

All this from a two-dimensional painting, a series of brushstrokes in oil. Nadine smiled to herself. Sewell definitely had a unique talent. In fact, it occurred to her, he had two: painting and sex.

It was possible, of course, that what she was doing was superimposing her own views and feelings about Sewell on to the pictures. Perhaps that's why she felt she knew what the brunette was feeling so accurately. But that did not explain the emotional nexus between the three characters, nor the emotion she felt emanating from the other pictures.

As quietly as she could, she padded down the bare floorboards of the staircase. It was only when she reached the carpeted hallway again that she was struck with the idea that the brunette must be more than just a model for Sewell and so, equally, the blonde. The situations he painted were hardly the stuff of a normal life class. On the other hand she didn't know enough about how artists worked to be sure of this assumption. They might well be models who Sewell painted from life, using his imagination to put them into the situations and express their feelings.

Another question was prompted by this thought. All the pictures she had seen involved threesomes, two women and one man. Was that situation real or imaginary? Did Sewell regularly indulge himself in this way?

Would she end up immortalised in one of Sewell's canvasses? Nadine wondered as she tip-toed back into the bedroom. Did she want that? It was an interesting prospect. But then Sewell was an interesting prospect for many reasons, not least that he was undoubtedly the most attractive man she had met in years, to say nothing of the best lover.

The bedroom floor creaked as she walked in but Sewell did not wake. He was lying on his back, his body covered by the single white sheet, the black triangle of his pubic hair outlined beneath it.

Nadine saw no point in waking him. She picked up the white silk teddy and drew it over her body, being as quiet as she could. She pulled on her blouse and skirt. She stepped into her shoes and stooped to pick up her ruined tights by the side of the bed. As she did so, something caught her eye sticking out from under the cream vallance that surrounded the base of the bed. It was a corner of black silk. She pulled it out and found herself holding a silk negligee trimmed in delicate lace. It was quite obvious that it had been hastily hidden under the bed. Nadine remembered Sewell going upstairs for a few minutes when they'd first got to the house.

Nadine felt anger rise in her like a fever. Her first reaction was to wake Sewell and have it out with him but she stopped herself. Anger implied that she cared and she didn't want to give him the satisfaction of seeing her out of control. Besides, she hadn't asked him if he was married or involved with anyone and hadn't actually given a damn if he was. She'd come here for one reason only. It was her fault. She should have asked.

Calmly she picked up the tights and walked out of the bedroom. As if to prove something to herself she went into the bathroom. Behind the sculpted lines of the washhand basin was a mirrored cupboard. She opened it. One shelf was littered with female toiletries, nail varnish, make-up, a box of Tampax, some quite obviously stuffed into the cupboard hurriedly.

Nadine left the cupboard door open, just as she'd left the black negligee draped across the bedroom carpet. She wanted Sewell to know that she knew.

Not caring about the noise now she went downstairs, picked up her handbag from the hall table where she'd left it last night and opened the front door. With every ounce of strength she possessed she slammed the door shut behind her. At the same time, just as emphatically, slamming the door shut on the startling emotions Sewell had stirred within her.

'So what did he say?'

'Nothing.'

'He couldn't have said nothing. He must have said something.'

'I didn't see him.'

'Why not?'

'There was no need. He delivered the graphics. They were fine. They were better than fine, they were fantastic. I'm halfway to getting the account . . .'

'And?'

'And I sent him my cheque for five hundred pounds as agreed. End of story. So I had to sleep with him as well. It was worth it.'

'Aren't you curious?'

'About what?'

'About who she was?'

'I don't care, Babs.'

'Oh come on, this is me you're talking to. You've spent the last half-an-hour talking to me about him.'

'I mean I don't care who *she* is. I guess she's one of the women in the paintings.'

They were sitting in the bar of the Park Curzon Hotel in Mayfair. It had been a hot, humid day and they were glad of the super-chilled air that the hotel's air-conditioner pumped out so efficiently.

Barbara Geddes was a tall and striking redhead, the sort of woman men look at with greedy eyes but, on reflection, fear. Her personality – open, honest, and perhaps a little brash – was too daunting for all but the most confident of men. As was her physique. As well as being nearly six foot tall Barbara, though not overweight, had a big strong-looking body that matched her height. Nadine could imagine her as an Amazonian warrior queen, bare-breasted with animal skins draped around her hips, holding the reigns of a chariot in one hand and a sword the size of Excalibur in the other.

She wore clothes that emphasised this appearance and tonight was no exception, a leopardskin-print body in a material that shone as though it were wet, clinging to every contour of her torso, while her legs were just as tightly encased in leggings in the same print. Brown lace-up calf-length boots, with spiky heels that made no concession to her height, clad her feet.

Soft wavy hair framed a strong face with a straight nose and a firm jawline. Her large eyes were an unusual dark green, the whites as pure as fresh snow.

'So what are you going to do?' Barbara asked, indicating to a passing waiter that they needed refills for their champagne cocktails.

'What should I do? Call him and ask him if he'd like to fuck me again next time his wife's away?'

'You don't know he's married,' Barbara said.

'Let's change the subject shall we?'

'He's really got under your skin, hasn't he?'

'It's the first time I've ever done it, Babs. The first time I've ever thrown myself at a man like that. There was just something about him. And, Jesus, he was so good in bed.'

'You didn't tell me that bit. Go on.' Barbara leaned forward in the comfortable armchair.

Just as Nadine was about to speak the waiter arrived with their drinks. Nadine waited while he picked up the two empty glasses on the table in front of them, replaced the frilled paper coasters stamped with the logo of the hotel, and set the full glasses down. For a moment, as it was so obvious he had interrupted their conversation, there was an awkward silence.

'Thank you,' Barbara said.

The waiter nodded and hurried away.

'So?'

'It's hard to describe. It wasn't any one thing. It was everything. Everything he did. He was so hard.'

'His cock, you mean?'

'His cock and his body. But the odd thing was that the paintings were just like the way he fucked.' She would normally have said 'made love' but did not want to use the word 'love' in the context of Sewell. 'There was something incredibly sexy about them and I don't think it was just because of what he'd done to me.'

'He's talented then?'

'Very. I think he knows he's a very attractive man and he plays on it. But I don't think he knows what a good painter he is. We've got to stop talking about him. It's over, finished. I'm not going to have an affair with a married man.'

'But you'd have gone to bed with him if he'd told you?'

'Yes, I would. Once. But only once. I wouldn't have an affair.'

'Rubbish.'

'It is not. When Gordon ran off with that little bitch from Grays I swore I'd never be the other woman.'

'He didn't run off, Nadine.'

'He did.'

'He didn't fall, he was pushed.'

'He fell for that little bimbo. He couldn't wait to get into her knickers – though what he used beats me. I always had trouble keeping him awake, let alone erect.'

They laughed.

'So that's that?'

'Definitely.'

'You'll have to see him again.'

'Not really. He's done the work. If I get the account there'll be some major changes but that's all. I can cope with that.'

'Well, as a matter of record, I think you're making a mistake. I think you should put up a fight. There aren't many men like that.'

'He's got someone, Barbara. As far as I'm concerned that's the end of the story. Aren't we all supposed to be sisters?'

'Balls!'

'We'd better get going, hadn't we?' Nadine looked at her watch, a Cartier tank she had brought herself as a birthday present two years ago. 'What time does it start?'

'Eight.'

'It's eight-thirty now.'

'Nobody who's anybody gets there till nine.'

Barbara was the press officer at the advertising agency where Nadine worked, though they had known each other since university. Barbara had been sent down in her second year for repeatedly failing to do any work whatsoever. Nadine had suggested her friend to the company when the job became vacant, Barbara having pursued a moderately successful career as a journalist. Since then Barbara had gone from strength to strength, the chumminess and good companionship required of a press officer, the ability to laugh and make others laugh, while at the same time selling them a nicely placed story, came naturally to her. She had obtained millions of pounds worth of free advertising for the agency's clients and was highly paid as a result.

Tonight she had been invited to the launch of a biography written by a tabloid journalist she had done a lot of business with and, as it promised to be a glamorous affair, she had asked Nadine along too. The subject of the biography was Anne Armstrong, probably the most successful English star currently working in Hollywood, who was married to Antony Leech, a film director whose last movie had made more money than the budget of a medium-sized South American republic.

Nadine had accepted the invitation with alacrity. It was exactly what she wanted after her night with Sewell, a chance to dress up and flirt outrageously with a dozen men and maybe, just maybe, in the mood she was in, do more than flirt. She was wearing a skin-tight red dress in a shimmering moiré, her shoulders bare apart from thin spaghetti straps. Its tightness compressed her breasts into a dramatic cleavage and showed off her narrow waist, while the comparatively short skirt displayed a great deal of her long legs, sheathed in glassy black tights.

They finished their champagne and spent five minutes in the marbled ladies room of the hotel, adjusting their hair and dabbling with their make-up until they were satisfied they could face the world. They stepped outside to the waiting limousine, a Daimler Princess, that Barbara had decided the advertising agency would pay for.

The launch was being held in the Senior Common Room of the Royal College of Art where, it so happened, Anne Armstrong had spent two years before her interest turned from fine art to acting.

The car glided smoothly around Hyde Park Corner and down through Knightsbridge into Kensington Gore. As they approached the Albert Hall they could see a chaos of people and cars with policemen cordoning off a large area around the main entrance to the RCA. Television lights bathed the whole scene in a harsh white light as flashbulbs popped and a crowd milled around on the edges of the cordon in the hope of glimpsing one of the star guests. Their driver moved into a line of cars waiting to be admitted and they were waved through as Barbara pressed her gold-embossed invitation to the back window.

Ahead of them a white Cadillac limousine disgorged a young man in jeans and a white T-shirt. On his arm was a voluptuous girl in turquoise satin flares and a white frilly blouse tied in a knot below her breasts. Though Nadine did not know who they were, the photographers pressed forward eagerly and demanded intimate poses which the couple appeared happy to strike. They had no difficulty either, in persuading the girl to display more of her ample, unhaltered, bosom.

Seeing the Daimler approach, the photographers pressed forward again only to recede rapidly as Barbara and Nadine stepped onto the pavement. Obviously they were not worth wasting film on.

The two women walked into the long foyer, hung

47

with examples of the current students' works, and over to the lifts. Despite the fact that Nadine was by no means short, Barbara seemed to tower over her friend.

As the lift doors opened on the top floor the buzz of conversation hit them like a wave of heat. The room was packed with celebrities, Nadine recognised so many faces it was impossible to remember all their names.

Taking two glasses of champagne from a waitress dressed in a black leotard that had been printed on the front to look like a man's dress shirt and black bow-tie, the two friends drank a toast.

'Here's to a good time.'

'I'll drink to that.'

They circulated and Barbara introduced Nadine to the author who in turn introduced them both to Anne Armstrong, a small, painfully thin blonde with a pretty face, and to Antony Leech, her even more diminutive husband.

The conversation sparkled but as the banter was thrown around the small group Nadine found it hard to join in. She did not seem to be able to get herself into the swing of things. It was the first time she had gone out since her night with Sewell and she was surprised to discover that he haunted her like a spectre at the feast – she was staring at the huge oil of Belshazzar's Feast that dominated the Senior Common Room. Each time she saw a man from the back with straight black hair she expected it to be Sewell and each time they turned around she was disappointed. She knew rationally there was no reason for him to be there but that didn't matter.

Annoyed with herself, she drank more champagne than she intended. The walls of the Common Room were all hung with examples of successful former students' work. Nadine drifted away from Barbara's group and studied the paintings, comparing the impression they made on her with what she had seen in Sewell's studio. Only the compressed and twisted energy of Francis Bacon came anywhere near to the impact Sewell's work had had on her.

Sewell again, she thought angrily. In the last three days since their night together, was there an hour in which she hadn't thought about him? Damn him. Damn him to hell.

Quite deliberately she looked around the room. Perhaps it was the champagne but she decided that what she needed was a man. That was the only thing that was going to get Sewell off her mind, another man. At this moment she didn't even particularly care who.

'You'll do,' she said, intending the remark to be under her breath but in fact saying it quite loud.

'Sorry?'

She had found herself standing alongside a small group of people as they took glasses of champagne from one of the waitresses. She was looking straight at a neatly dressed and tidy young man with fair hair and a fresh, open face, the sort of man who looked as though he would have the greatest trouble in telling a lie. That was a proposition she would put to the test.

'Are you married?'

'No,' he said smiling at her and coming a little closer.

'Living with someone?'

'No.'

Neither of these answers caused him to blush or blink in any way and Nadine felt reassured.

'Why do you ask?' he said.

'Because I think you're very attractive.'

'Thank you.'

As she looked at him she thought there was something familiar about his face.

'Do I know you?'

'No. I'm an actor. Everyone makes that mistake. I'm not famous enough to be recognised by name but everyone thinks they know me because I've been in their front rooms on the telly.'

'I don't watch telly.'

'Films.'

'You've been in films?'

'I was in Antony Leech's last epic.'

'Haven't seen it.'

'Charles Denbigh,' he said extending his hand. The group he had been with had all melted away.

'Nadine Davies.' She extended her hand and he took it selfconsciously.

'And what do you do?'

'Advertising.'

'Perhaps you can help get me into voice-overs.'

'Always on the make.'

'Sorry?'

She realised that was incredibly rude. She pulled herself together and put her half-empty champagne glass down very firmly. She was not going to get drunk as a way of getting back at Sewell. That was silly.

'I need a glass of water,' she said.

'Shall I get you one? Are you all right?'

'I'm fine, I just need some water.'

He turned away and forced a path through the crowd. It swallowed him up but in a couple of minutes he appeared from an entirely different direction bearing a large glass of water.

'Here.'

Nadine drank it all. 'Thank you, very gallant.'

Charles smiled. He was not tall and he almost had to look up at Nadine. His face had the air of an eager little boy. He appeared nervous. He was the complete opposite of Sewell.

'Gallantry should be rewarded, shouldn't it?'

'Are you going to give me a medal?'

'Better than that . . .' What was happening to her? She felt her body pulsing with excitement as it had that night with Sewell. It was sexual excitement. She wanted to have sex. She needed to have sex. It was not a feeling she could ever remember having before. Sex had always been very low on her agenda because it had always been less than satisfactory. But after what she'd experienced with Sewell it seemed her body had moved it up her list of priorities.

She felt coquettish and wicked. It was a delicious feeling. She took Charles by the arm.

'Where are we going?' he said.

She didn't answer until they were standing by the lifts and she had pressed the call button. 'I'm going home,' she said quietly. 'I'd like you to come with me. I need you to fuck me, Charles.'

Charles grinned and blushed at the same time.

'Why me?' he said.

'Does there have to be a reason?'

'No, I suppose not.' He looked like a man who had been given a death sentence rather than an invitation to a beautiful woman's bed. He put his champagne glass down as the lift doors slid open.

'Well?' she said.

She saw him making his decision. His expression changed. 'Let's go.'

'Have you got a car?'

'Yes, it's parked round the back.'

'Good.'

She held his arm in the lift almost as though he might run away, grasping it tightly. There was none of the hardness of muscle that she'd noticed in Sewell's arms. Sewell again, damn him!

It took twenty minutes to drive to Nadine's Victorian terraced house in Fulham. By the time they had got there the effects of the champagne had worn off completely and she felt entirely sober. But she was no less excited. She had never done anything like this in her life before and it was exhilarating. Three days ago she had gone to bed with a man she had known for only a few hours. Now this. It seemed a natural progression.

'Do you want another drink?' she said as she closed the front door.

'No thank you,' he said, 'but don't let me stop you.' He looked distinctly nervous and uneasy.

Without any hesitation Nadine walked up the straight staircase at the end of the hall. She heard Charles following and knew he would be getting a good view of her firm buttocks, tightly covered by the red moiré. She led the way into her bedroom.

The bedroom was decorated in dark blues. The carpet and walls were the same colour, the curtains a diamond pattern in a lighter shade and the counterpane was made from the same material. The double bed was an iron bedstead with brass ends.

'Let me hang up your jacket,' she said.

He slipped his jacket off and she hung it on a hanger on the back of the bedroom door. It was a good material and an expensive make.

'Are you the sort of man who is put off by women taking the initiative?' She said on the edge of the bed.

'I don't think so. It's never happened to me before, not so . . .'

'Blatantly?' she suggested.

'Yes.'

The natural thing to do would have been to let him kiss her, but she didn't want that, not yet at least. She didn't want a kiss to become a fumbling embrace, hands pulling at clothes, in a desperate attempt to expose the genitals, the fumbling followed by quick copulation and instant regret. As this was all a social experiment, and a psychological one too, she wanted something far more precise.

Her dress fastened down the side under her arm. She stood up and pulled down the metal tongue of the zip; the tight material parted allowing her to slip off the spaghetti straps and let the dress fall to the floor. She was wearing a lacy black strapless bra that pushed her breasts up and together so they ballooned out of its cups, and matching panties under the sheer, shimmering tights.

Her heart was beating fast. She could hear it thumping, the blood in her ears carrying its vibration. She stepped out of the dress and stooped to pick it up, hanging it on the back of the door over his jacket. Slowly she reached behind her back and unclipped her bra. With no straps to hold it in place the black lace fell away immediately, her breasts quivering at their sudden release.

'You're very beautiful,' Charles said. 'This is like a dream.'

'A wet dream?' What was happening to her? She would never have made a remark like that in normal circumstances. But it did not make her blush. In fact it emboldened her. Like an actress trying out a new role to see how she would play it, she tested her next line. 'Do I make you hard?'

'Yes.'

That was what she was doing, playing a role, the role of a vamp. There was a small mirror on one wall and she glimpsed herself in it. She hardly recognised what she saw, a semi-naked wanton standing in front of a total stranger, the expression on her face defiant, exhilarated and determined.

She walked around Charles and came up behind him. She sunk her mouth onto his neck above his collar and kissed him lightly as her hands ran down over his silk tie to the fly of his trousers. He hadn't lied. She felt the hardness of his erection trapped in the folds of material.

Nadine began unbuttoning his shirt.

'Can't I do that?' he said.

'I'll do the shirt, you take the tie.'

He pulled the tie and yanked it free of his collar. She opened the buttons then began tugging it out of his trousers. Her fingers found the zip of his fly and pulled it down.

She broke away from him and allowed him to do the rest as she stripped the counterpane and bedding off the bed until all that was left was the bottom sheet. She sat on the edge of the bed and watched as he kicked off his shoes, stripped off his socks, then pulled down his trousers and black briefs together. His cock sprung out. He wasn't circumcised and his foreskin bulged over his glans. His body was lean and slender. She thought that if she squeezed him hard he might break.

For the first time he took the initiative. He sat next to her on the edge of the bed, turned her head towards him with his hand on her cheek and kissed her on the mouth, his hand sliding down to cup her breast. He pushed his tongue into her mouth then allowed hers to push it back and return the compliment. Breaking away he dropped to his knees in front of her and eased her left foot out of her shoe. He massaged it with his fingers kneading her instep then brought the foot up to his mouth and kissed her toes. He repeated the process on the right foot.

'That's nice,' she said.

'Beautiful legs,' he muttered as his mouth kissed

the nylon on top of her foot, before putting it down.

Slowly and deliberately Nadine moved her legs apart on either side of him, exposing the crotch of her black panties under the tights. She saw Charles staring at it.

'That's lovely,' he said.

He stood up. 'Get onto the bed,' he said.

She obeyed, laying back in the middle of the bed, her head on the pillows, then spread her legs again, nudging the left up against his erection.

He stared at her intently, his eyes moving all over her body. She felt herself pulse in response. Slipping her hand under the waistband of her tights she ran it down her belly and under her panties until the tip of her middle finger was poised at the crease of her sex. She allowed her finger to delve deeper, parting her labia to search for her clitoris.

'Does that excite you?' she asked. There was no need to specify what 'that' meant.

'Yes, very much.'

'Mm . . .' Her finger found its objective. Her clit was already engorged. 'Oh, so good,' she said. And it was. She was still giving a performance, still flaunting her body in a way she had never done before but that did not mean the sensations she was feeling were not real. Far from it. Her body was crawling with excitement. For a moment she considered going all the way and letting him watch her masturbate. That would be another first, letting a man watch her do that. It wouldn't take much. But she resisted.

Instead she pulled her finger away and cupped

both her breasts in her hands. Her nipples were as
hard as stone and felt strangely cold, though the
rest of her body was warm.

Charles bent over her and grasped the waistband
of her tights, pulling them down over her hips. He
caught the waist of the panties too and tugged them
both down together. She co-operated, raising her
buttocks off the bed so he could roll both garments
down over her hips and her long legs.

He threw the nylon aside and knelt on the bed
beside her. His hands caressed the bare flesh of her
thighs. It was creamy and smooth. She parted her
legs again and allowed him to see her sex for the
first time. He stared at it intently, his gaze provoking
her. She felt as though her labia were swelling,
enjoying their freedom after being constricted for so
long. She knew she was wet and wondered if he could
see it.

His hands, both hands now, smoothed up along
her legs, spreading them further apart, until they
were right at the top, where her thighs dimpled
under the crease of the pelvis. His fingertips pressed
against the soft supple flesh, pulling it from either
side so that her sex lips were pulled apart too. There
was a slight sibilant squelch and Nadine shuddered.

Charles's hands stopped moving. He held her
thighs apart and stared into her vagina. It glistened.
He looked up into her eyes as if for some sort of
reassurance: it was all happening so fast he could
hardly believe it. Nadine stared back at him fiercely
letting him see the excitement dancing in her eyes.

He dipped his head down to her sex, his fingertips

still holding her apart. His tongue lapped out to touch the little nut of her clitoris. It was like being touched by a live electric wire. Nadine felt a shock of pleasure.

His tongue tapped on her clitoris like a tiny hammer, making Nadine gasp. She was wound up so tightly she knew at any minute she would start to unravel, her physical state being fed not only by what Charles was doing to her body but by her mind – by what she had done.

'You'll make me come,' she moaned.

He didn't stop, answering by tapping a little bit more powerfully, then moving his tongue down to her vagina, where it traced the circumference of her opening, stretching the scarlet flesh first in one direction then another as if testing its elasticity.

'Oh God, Charlie,' she gasped, congratulating herself on her choice of man. 'That's so good.'

Was it simply that he was good at doing this? Or was she over-sensitised by everything that had happened to her? Whichever it was, her body was throbbing, the first stirrings of orgasm well advanced.

'Don't stop,' she begged suddenly afraid he'd pull away. She'd give him pleasure later but for the moment this was too good. She wanted to come on his tongue. He did exactly what she hoped he would do and went back to her clitoris, this time licking it with long slow strokes, pushing it up and down, his tongue hot, pliant and insistent. She could feel her whole sex was wet, her juices merging with his saliva.

Everything narrowed down. The world was

reduced to the movement of his tongue on her clitoris, each stroke making her whole body shudder, taking her higher until she reached an imaginary plateau, on some precipice of feeling. Her eyes were closed. In her mind she saw herself in the mirror, standing in her tights and high heels. She saw the glint of excitement in her eyes at her daring. She squirmed her sex against Charles's mouth. She felt his hands move and fingers plunged into her not at all gently, up into her sex, until the knuckles of his hand pressing against her labia prevented deeper penetration.

Between cause and effect there seemed to be an inifinity of time. Everything stopped, the world stood still and then, as her sex contracted around his fingers, it seemed to explode. Colour, light and sensation shot out from every nerve and her body shook, her head tossing from side to side, her muscles in spasm. But amidst all this physical tumult, even as the storm raged through her body, there was part of her that was still, a part that stared calmly into the dark hooded eyes of John Sewell. The spectre had returned.

The storm passed, the waves of sensation ebbed away, the pounding blood in her veins returned to a normal pulse. Nadine opened her eyes as Charles straightened up, his lips and chin wet with her juices. For an instance she was confused that it was not John Sewell's face that greeted her.

'What's the matter?' Her confusion must have been obvious.

'Nothing,' she said.

She sat up and caught Charles's face in both hands, kissing him on the mouth and revelling in the taste of her own body. She realised it was the image of Sewell that had made her come and she cursed him again.

'Stand up,' she said. It came out as a command.

Charles kissed her thighs again lightly then got to his feet, his erection sticking out in front of him. Nadine sat on the edge of the bed and pulled him towards her so he was standing between her knees. Grasping his cock firmly in one hand she jerked his foreskin back. He moaned. His glans was as smooth as a plum. Before her eyes it swelled. She wrapped her arms around his waist then slid them down to his small buttocks. She opened her mouth and swallowed his cock, plunging forward until it was crammed tightly into the back of her throat.

She chewed on it. She sucked on it, withdrawing slightly so she could move her tongue over the rim of the glans and up to the slit of the urethra, trying to push the tip of her tongue inside it. As she did this, she worked her hand around his legs and grasped the sac of his balls. She sucked hard again and squeezed his balls tightly pulling the sac down away from his body. She was trying to provoke him.

She knew what she wanted, exactly what she wanted. It was an invocation to appease the spectre at the feast.

Pulling away from him, his cock glistening with her saliva, she got onto the bed on all fours, pointing her buttocks at Charles. The mirror was on the side wall, not at the foot of the bed as it had been with

Sewell so she had positioned herself across the bed. That didn't matter. What mattered was that she could put her head up at right angles to her spine and see herself in the glass, see her body and her breasts hanging down, see her buttocks and see Charles looking at her, looking at the long slit of her sex.

As she'd hoped it would, something snapped in him. He threw himself onto the bed behind her, pushed his cock down between her labia and into the gate of her sex. She was so wet his penetration was effortless sliding up into her until she could feel his stomach against her buttocks, her hot, wet, silky vagina melting over him, clinging to him, sucking him in.

'Yes,' she moaned.

He dug his hands into her hips and used them to pull her back onto him. Nadine let her head fall for a moment, sensations flooding through her body, her earlier orgasm immediately revived, her nerves tingling with anticipation. She closed her eyes and let the feelings wash over her.

Charles stroked into her, his strength belying his appearance. His rhythm was perfect for her. She felt her body tense, her nerves knitting together rapidly to become one whole, her consciousness of everything else but the phallus inside her drifting into the mists of passion.

Then slowly she raised her head and opened her eyes, managing to control her body. She looked directly into the mirror. She could see Charles behind her, his face a picture of concentration and effort, his eyes riveted to her buttocks, watching his cock rearing in and out of her body. She saw her own face just as taut and strained but she saw the face of the petite brunette too, the face she had seen in the painting, the expression of ecstasy an exact match for her own. Then it was not Charles who was fucking her but Sewell. *Sewell*. God, he'd felt so hard, so strong. Charles's cock was a slender imitation. But that didn't matter because as she looked into the mirror and saw Sewell's knowing smile she could feel his cock too, stretching her, using her, pounding into her deeper than any man had been.

Her orgasm flooded over over. Images, like snapshots projected on a screen, flashed into her mind as if triggered by the explosion of feeling. As her body shuddered, her nerves jangled and her muscles spasmed, her mind saw the brunette's face in the mirror again and the face of the blonde alongside her.

Charles's body shuddered. Her orgasm had been so intense and her sex contracted so fiercely he had been unable to do anything but wait till her crisis was over. Then, as the silky hand that gripped him so tightly, at last relaxed, he pushed forward gently. There was no need to do more. He felt his cock throb and then it was jerking wildly and his hot semen was spattering into Nadine's body.

He moaned softly. To Nadine it sounded like a cry of a lost soul who could not find his way home.

Chapter Three

It was a beautiful day. The last three days had been hot and humid but today a light breeze had brought cooler air that, even in central London, seemed to be scented with flowers.

The garage where Nadine parked her car was a short walk from her office in Frith Street. She had walked the streets of Soho a thousand times and been almost totally unaware of her surroundings, of the peep shows and sleazy clubs with big-breasted women outside touting for business. She had never stopped to look at the magazines piled into the windows of the sex shops en route or the scantily clad mannequins wearing the latest in erotic lingerie, or the shelves of dildoes and vibrators and other 'marital aids' as they were euphemistically called.

That had changed. Now she found herself examining these windows carefully, looking at each item. The purpose of some, of the phallus-shaped dildos and leather handcuffs, of the blindfolds and ball gags, were perfectly obvious. Other items were more difficult to place.

The desire to go inside had grown irresistible. It had come, she knew, from trying to imagine what one of the large cream plastic dildos would feel like inside her. The thought had made her sex throb so strongly she had walked away from the window rapidly. But she could not walk away from the thought and tonight she had decided to be brave. It was an experiment, she told herself, and there was no harm in it.

She knew, of course, why she was in the mood to experiment, as she'd experimented with Charles. It was because she found it hard not to think about sex, as hard as she found it not to think about Sewell. Like the Sleeping Beauty, she seemed to have been woken from a long slumber, as far as sex was concerned at least, by a handsome Prince. And now she found it impossible to get back to sleep again.

Looking around at least twice to satisfy herself there was no one she knew on the street, she pushed aside the swinging multi-coloured plastic strips that formed the entrance to the sex shop.

Four men's eyes swivelled onto her immediately. There were two men behind a makeshift wooden counter on which was perched a very old-fashioned cash register, and two customers, both browsing among racks of plastic-covered magazines, most, as far as she could see, displaying girls with gigantic bosoms. The customers turned away from her quickly, hurrying behind a rack of magazines in the centre of the shop from which they could not be seen.

Nadine spotted the shelves where the dildoes were displayed. There appeared to be every size and colour and type. There were ones shaped like an extended finger and thumb only bigger and others the size of a little finger. There were big black ones with balls and, most popular of all it seemed, cream ones with a knob at one end which presumably switched the vibrator on.

She quickly selected the one she had seen in the window. It was neatly packed in a red box.

'Do you want the batteries?' the man said as she put it down on the counter next to the till.

'Sorry?'

'Batteries? It works on batteries. They're not included.'

She felt sure the batteries in this shop would be double the cost of batteries elsewhere but she didn't want to have to march into Boots and measure the dildo for the right size. 'Yes, please,' she said.

'We've got the Chinese balls on special offer,' the other man said. He didn't look up from his copy of *The Sun*.

'No thanks,' she said.

Neither man appeared phased by serving a woman. The first man put the box in a brown bag with two batteries.

'Fifteen ninety-five,' he said.

Nadine gave him a twenty-pound note. The cash register jingled as its drawer sprung open. He handed her the change.

'Have a nice day,' he said, apparently with no hint of irony.

Nadine shot from the shop and down the street checking that again there was no one to observe her guilty secret. She reached her car and put the package on the front seat.

As she started the car and put in the clutch the movement of her legs made her aware of her sex.

She knew instinctively that she was moist. She felt her clitoris pulse.

'This is ridiculous,' she said aloud but the feeling did not go away.

It had not gone away by the time she arrived home and let herself into the front door, the brown paper bag clutched in her hand.

She picked up the post but didn't open it. She walked upstairs unbuttoning her blouse as she went. It had been hot in the car and she needed a shower. In her bedroom she stripped off the rest of her clothes quickly and went into her bathroom. It was the coolest room in her house and the chill was welcome. She reached into the shower cubicle and turned on the powerful shower she had installed as a special luxury. It had a two-and-a-half horsepower motor hidden in the panelling somewhere and delivered a jet of water that was difficult to stand up against. But Nadine loved that, particularly on a day like today. She waited until the water was lukewarm then stepped into the glass cubicle and let the spray cascade off her body.

She reached for the soap and lathered her body generously. It was only when she came to her breasts that she felt a jolt of sensation. They were sensitive, extra sensitive, her nipples puckered under the shower of water, responding as though she were in bed with a lover. She moved the soap down to her pubic hair and felt the same reaction. Her body appeared to have its own agenda.

Washing the soap away she turned the water off and climbed out into the cool of the bathroom again.

She towelled herself down, being careful to avoid
her nipples and her sex, but she knew she was only
fooling herself if she thought they could be ignored.

She went back into the bedroom naked and hung
up her clothes. The brown paper bag lay on the
counterpane.

Nadine had masturbated regularly in her life,
though not frequently. Like sex itself, she had never
found it a particularly satisfying experience. It was
pleasant but not more than that. She had not
masturbated since she'd met Sewell.

She picked up the bag and extracted the red box.
The batteries fell on the bed. She opened the box
and pulled out a white plastic case. She held the
dildo in her hand. She felt her sex throb.

Unscrewing the end, following the diagram on the
box, she pushed the batteries inside the hollow tube.
As she screwed the knob back into place the vibrator
came alive and she dropped it as though it had
suddenly turned into a snake. It lay on the bed,
humming loudly.

Picking it up she felt the vibrations making her
fingers tingle. Tentatively, she touched the tip of
the phallus against her nipple. It was a pleasant
sensation but nothing more.

She traced the phallus down over her navel
holding it as though it were a pen. As it nuzzled into
her soft fleece of pubic hair she felt the vibrations
reach down into her sex. She looked into the mirror
and watched as her hand pushed the tip of the dildo
into the crease of her sex.

She was seized by a delicious sensation. The dildo

seemed to find its own way to her clitoris and the vibration agitated it so beautifully that Nadine gasped.

She sat on the bed and then changed her mind. She pulled back the counterpane and lay on her back. Bending her legs at the knee so she could put her feet flat on the sheet, Nadine opened her legs wide. With her spare hand she fingered her labia and touched her clitoris. She felt an immediate jolt of pleasure.

She held her labia open with the fingers of her left hand then pushed the tip of the dildo down between her legs again. It homed into her clitoris with breathtaking accuracy. Now the sensation was so sharp Nadine caught her breath.

She knew she could come like this, come wonderfully, just by holding the dildo against her clitoris. But she didn't want the experiment to end just yet.

With one finger she explored the opening of her sex. As she'd suspected, it was wet. It had been wet since the sex shop. She traced the dildo down and guided it to the entrance of her vagina. Its vibrations still affected her clitoris but her labia were vibrating too and emitting little trills of feeling she had never felt before.

She pushed the dildo into her sex, just an inch or so at first. It was wide and stretched her. She could feel the cold plastic but most of all she felt its hardness, harder than any cock she'd ever had, harder even than Sewell. She prodded it deeper. Strangely the deeper it went the more the vibrations seemed to increase, making her whole body tremble. It was half in now and she was feeling another flush of pleasure. She could come like this too, come with the dildo inside her. She squeezed her sex around it and felt it yield not at all. Its inflexibility thrilled her again.

Almost before she realised what was happening, and certainly before she could do anything to stop it, an orgasm had started to churn in her body, demanding completion. She was astonished at its intensity. There seemed to be a direct connection between her sex and her clitoris, both vibrating to the same frequency.

Instinctively, she jammed the dildo deep into her body, as deep as it would go, as deep as Sewell had been inside her. There the vibrations reached a pitch, discovering nerves at the neck of her womb that she'd never felt before, making her feel penetrated and invaded, making her clitoris throb uncontrollably. She used a finger of her other hand to grope for her clitoris as she held the dildo deep inside her. There was no need to move it, no need to pretend it was a cock and stroke it in and out. The vibrations were enough. She held herself tightly, her whole hand covering the delta of her sex, holding it as if to ensure the orgasm that was breaking over the head of the cream plastic phallus, could not escape. She was crushing her clitoris against her pubic bone but it still vibrated, sending shock waves out in a spiralling circle until the orgasm slowly ebbed away.

As suddenly as if a switch had been thrown, Nadine's energy was spent. The dildo was still inside her but she did not have the strength to hold it there and she dropped her hands to her sides. Gradually, with infinite slowness, she felt her body expel it, the silky velvet walls of her sex coming together to push the intruder out. As it travelled downwards she realised that the motion would make her come again as the plastic member was finally jettisoned from her body. And that's what happened.

'God . . .' Nadine cried aloud as the phallus shot out and her body shuddered out of control again.

What was happening to her?

She finally summoned the energy to get up off the bed. She put the dildo away decisively in the drawer of her bedside table, pulled on a light cotton robe and went down to the kitchen to get something to eat.

The cold light of the morning after her night with Charles had brought recrimination and regret. She had told herself she was behaving like a love-sick teenager, on the rebound from one man and using another. Not only using but abusing, abusing herself in the process.

And now this. Sewell, in the words of the song, had got under her skin and there appeared to be no easy way to get him out again.

In the last few days Nadine's attitude had changed. Not that her obsession with him had got any less. It hadn't. Her mind had drifted into thinking about him whenever she had a spare moment, and sometimes when she didn't, and in the evenings she had lain alone in bed running and re-running in her mind everything that had happened that evening like an endless video loop.

But as she laid cheese, salad and a bottle of white wine on the small kitchen table, a thought occurred to her. She had jumped to the conclusion that Sewell was married or living with somebody. But what if he wasn't? What if the negligee had belonged to some casual girlfriend? Certainly there were toiletries in the bathroom that belonged to a woman but how carefully had she examined them? They may have been odd items left by a woman for emergencies. And, though she hadn't seen all of the house there was, she thought, nothing much she could pinpoint to indicate a woman in residence.

As she ate her meal, she began to convince herself – and that, of course, is what she desperately wanted to do – that she had found Sewell guilty on very little evidence. She had been the prosecuting counsel, judge and jury. She had not even allowed him one word in his own defence. Sewell was a proud man, much too proud to call her, and she had refused to see him when he'd delivered the art work. There might well be a simple explanation. Should she at least give him a chance to explain? Didn't he deserve that much? Didn't *she*?

The sun broke through the trees at the back of the house as it set and bright sunlight filtered in through the Venetian blinds, catching her full in the face. She did not move.

It was extraordinary the impact Sewell had made on her life, however much she would have liked to deny it. No man had ever made her feel the way Sewell made her feel. He seemed to have stripped

71

away the protective coating of her life that she had tried so hard to build up and reduced her to a core element, the essential Nadine. It surprised her that so much of what was essential seemed to be concerned with sex.

She closed her eyes against the brightness of the sun. She could see his face, the strong lines of his jaw and the comma of hair falling over his forehead brushed back by a flick of the head. She could see his body, his chest and arms and thighs thick with muscle. She could see his penis, the smoothness of the glans, the hardness of the shaft, sprouting from the mat of his pubic hair.

She studied his cock, inspecting every detail. She could see it developing a little tear of fluid at the slit of the urethra. She could see the network of veins that surrounded it, some sticking out like the stems of ivy wrapped around a tree. She watched it as her lips closed around it.

No. She opened her eyes and blinked against the light. What was happening to her? It was a symptom of what Sewell had done to her. He had altered the balance of her life.

Before her marriage she couldn't honestly say sex had meant that much to her. Her one or two significant experiences had soon faded into the mists of time, obviously they had not been *that* significant. As for married life, Gordon had made it perfectly clear that his sexual appetites could be easily satisfied, or so it appeared. It suited Nadine not to have to perform any elaborate sexual rituals with her husband. She concentrated on her career and was quite content with what rapidly became, after the initial burst of enthusiasm, a weekly, then a monthly event.

It had come as a shock to her when she discovered that Gordon's sexual menu was a great deal more extensive and the petite blonde he had run off with was, according to Barbara who had confronted the girl on Nadine's behalf, subjected to a thorough going-over on any and every occasion that presented itself – in the back of cars, over his desk in the office, in the ladies toilet of a pub, four or five times a week more often than not. Even when they had first met Gordon had never displayed such energy with her.

The divorce had not really touched Nadine. She had got married too young and for the wrong reason – an insurance policy should her bid for a successful career fail – and she was not at all sorry to see the back of Gordon. She had been involved with one or two men since and had dutifully gone to bed with them. Equally dutifully she had experienced orgasm. The men had been carefully selected and were well trained in the modern mores of bedroom behaviour. They had indulged in extensive foreplay, manipulated her clitoris with hand and tongue, and held back their own gratification until they were absolutely certain she had achieved her own. Under such circumstances not to have reached a climax would have seemed churlish.

But her affairs had made little or no impact on her life. If she were honest with herself Nadine had regarded sex like an itch that had to be scratched.

2

Satisfying such an urge was momentarily pleasurable but no more.

Sewell had changed all that. Sex with him was a new experience. It was a combination of the physical and the mental. He had aroused her body, her nerves, her senses, in a way they had never been aroused before but, more than that, he had provoked and stimulated her mind, filling it with images and emotions that had moved her profoundly. She wasn't sure how he managed to do it. She could analyse his sexual technique to discover precisely how he'd made her body succumb, but she could not fathom how he had manipulated her mind. He had succeeded in wiping everything else away, all thought that did not involve sex and what he could do to her. Her orgasms had been a physical shock. He had touched something in her that she didn't know existed.

Of course it may be that she was ripe for it, that he had come into her life at precisely the right moment. That after suppressing it for so long, what she now craved was sex.

Whatever the cause, the beast that had lain for so long undisturbed and neglected had woken from its sleep and lumbered into her life to cause, unless she was very careful, complete havoc.

She hadn't the slightest idea what she was going to say.

'Hello?'

'Sewell?' Why hadn't she called him John? She thought of him as Sewell but the word sounded odd when she said it.

74

'Yes.'

'Nadine Davies.'

'Hello.'

She was listening for clues as to what his attitude to her might be. The 'Hello' sounded warm and friendly. But, on the other hand, he hadn't said 'How are you?'

'How are you?' she asked.

'Fine.' Again he did not reciprocate. He wasn't interested in her health or well-being. He wasn't making it easy for her.

'Did you get the cheque?'

'You know I did.'

'Brandlings are impressed. They're making a decision next week. You did excellent work.'

'I'm glad you were pleased.' Each statement he made gave her no opening to continue.

'I'm sure we'll get the account.' She couldn't think of anything else to say. Where was she going to start?

'Why did you walk out?' he asked.

The question was so unexpected it completely wrong-footed her.

'I . . . I was . . . you know why.'

'Because of what you found?'

'Yes.' She saw the lacy black negligee lying on the cream carpet where she'd left it.

'I'm not married,' he said answering the unasked question.

'What then?'

He ignored the question. 'Don't you think you should have given me chance to explain. After what happened.'

'What did happen? We had sex . . .'

'Nadine. Please. Do you fondly imagine two people do what we did and feel what we felt, as a matter of course? Don't tell me you didn't feel there was something special between us, something exceptional . . .'

Nadine's mouth was dry. She felt as though she had stopped breathing.

'That's why I was calling,' she improvised quickly.

'Why?'

'To give you a chance to explain.'

'Why did you leave it so long?'

'You could have called me.'

'Nadine, your secretary told me you didn't want to see me when I delivered the art work. I thought that was pretty conclusive.'

He was right of course. 'Yes. I'm sorry.'

He had taken her by surprise and she was completely on the defensive.

'Tonight then?'

'Tonight?'

'Come here at eight.' It was a statement not a question.

'Fine.'

'You remember the address?'

'Yes.'

'Bye.'

Nadine put the phone down. His reaction had been the last thing she had expected. She'd thought he would be sullen and unforthcoming or downright rude. She hadn't expected such an affirmation of her own feelings, a confirmation that what had occurred between them was as special for him as it had been for her. She'd assumed, with the sexual magnetism he exuded like a subtle scent, his sexual prowess had the same effect on all women. That he could reduce them all to jelly and get his own satisfaction along the way. It hadn't even occurred to her, such was her lack of confidence in these matters, that she'd been special too.

She sat back in her leather chair. Her office was in the corner of a big open-plan floor, divided from the rest of the desks by a thin partition of wood and glass, the latter extending from waist level to the ceiling, enabling her to see out. She watched the activity as assistants and secretaries scurried about. She had a meeting in half-an-hour with the creative director and needed a whole set of papers, the correlated returns from the latest market research which had been promised to her yesterday. Suddenly having to tell her boss that the figures were not yet available seemed dreadfully unimportant in the scale of things. For the first time in some years, it seemed, she had other, more pressing priorities.

She wasn't going to say anything, she wasn't even going to ask him about the negligee and the other things. She'd made that decision. She was determined she wasn't going to be wrong-footed again. It was up to him to explain, especially after what he'd said on the phone.

She had worked everything out as she'd prepared for the evening. She'd taken her bath, washed and dried her hair, applied a rather heavier make-up

77

than usual and chosen very carefully what she was going to wear, selecting her underwear with as much thought as her dress. She intended to be cool and objective. If he made no attempt to explain, if the phone call had just been a way of getting her back into his bed she would simply leave. Of course she wanted to have sex with him but it had to be on her terms. It was up to him.

As she parked her car outside his house Nadine felt perfectly calm. She checked her hair briefly in the rearview mirror and got out. Since talking to him on the phone she had managed to keep her feelings for Sewell well in check. She had an edge on him now, after what he'd revealed. She felt more confident of herself. That didn't mean she wanted him any less but she felt in control whereas before she had not. She would have no difficulty in leaving if his explanation was not good enough. Or at least that was the delusion from which she was suffering.

'Hi.'

He had opened the front door before she had rung the bell. Sewell's house was attached to others on either side but not terraced – the houses on either side being of a different design. It was what estate agents call a 'cottage' property, a small square Georgian house with a short front garden. It was situated on the fringes of Hampstead.

'Come in.'

With the exception of the hallway, Sewell had knocked down all the dividing walls on the ground floor to make a large living space that included the kitchen, dining, and sitting rooms. He showed her

78

in. She hadn't seen this room on her last visit.

Sewell's furniture was eclectic. He had a single sofa, a cavernous monster upholstered in a dark red. There was a set of antique spoon-backed chairs around a circular mahogany dining table but the occasional table in front of the sofa was made from layers of thick glass and ultra modern. There was a bookcase in one of the alcoves formed by the chimney breast filled to overflowing with books, most of them on art. None of the pictures on the walls, of which there were many, appeared to be Sewell's, not at least in the style Nadine had seen upstairs.

'I opened a bottle of champagne,' he said as he lead her to the sofa. There was a bottle of non-vintage champagne in an aluminium French wine cooler filled with ice and two modern champagne flutes on the glass table. 'You look lovely.'

'Thank you.' Nadine had chosen a simple black dress that left her shoulders and arms bare but showed no cleavage and covered her legs to the knee. 'This is a marvellous table.'

'Glass is a beautiful material. Do you know you can actually make chairs of it? It's incredibly strong.'

He poured the champagne and she chose not to sit on the sofa but in a black leather Eames chair next to it. He handed her one of the flutes and clinked his against the side of it.

'Cheers,' he said.

'Cheers, Sewell,' she said in just the right tone of voice, cool and detached just as she'd intended. She sipped the chilled wine which matched her mood.

He was wearing a pair of faded jeans and a beige

military style shirt. It was unbuttoned and Nadine could see the mat of black hair at his throat. She hadn't noticed before that several of the hairs were white. He sat on the corner of the vast sofa.

'When did you say you'll know about the Brandling account?'

'Next week. Wednesday, I think. I'm sure they'll like your ideas. They were very good.'

'But you didn't want to tell me that personally?'

'I . . .' He was putting her on the defensive again. 'I didn't realise you wanted to talk business.'

'I don't.'

'What do you want to talk about?' The effect Sewell had on her, the way those dark fathomless eyes looked at her, had not lessened. The impact was the same as when he'd first walked into her office. So far she was managing to keep herself under control. Her pulse was racing and she had to keep reminding herself to breath, but her voice was level and cool.

'You remember I said I was saving up for my retirement?'

'Yes.'

'It's very difficult . . . very private I suppose. My art, I mean. What I want to say through painting. I'm not ready to show my work to the public. Not yet. But I'd like you to see it.'

Nadine felt her control slipping. Once again it was the last thing she expected him to say. He was looking at her steadily, his eyes suggesting that he was revealing a dark secret to her that few had shared. Of course, she'd seen his painting already, had been privy to his unique talent but this was

80

definitely not the time to own up to that truth.

'I'd like that,' she said finding it impossible not to keep the warmth out of her voice.

'They may shock you.'

'Shock me? How?' She knew perfectly well how.

'They are a very personal statement.'

'What does that mean?'

'I'd better show you.'

He got up and extended his hand to help her up, as the Eames was particularly low. At some point in her intellectual preparations for the evening she had told herself she would not touch him before matters had been resolved but she automatically put out her hand and instantly wished she hadn't. Touching his hand was like plugging into an electric circuit, except it was not electricity that flowed between them but sex, a current of sensation so strong she snatched her hand away as though she had been stung.

Sewell appeared not to notice.

He led her to the stairs and she could feel his eyes on her legs as she walked up ahead of him. She was wearing black high-heeled shoes that shaped the muscles of her calves, slimming them to a slender oval. The Achilles tendon at the back of her ankles had pronounced hollows and her ankles themselves were narrow and thin. Perhaps she even swung her hips more than she would normally do, the dress clinging tightly to her pert, firm buttocks.

She went to the door of the attic, then realised she wasn't supposed to know where his paintings were.

'Clever,' he said before she could wander further down the hall.

'Clever?' she said innocently.

'Working out where the studio was.'

'This has to be it.'

He didn't question her any further, merely smiled and opened the door. This time he went first up the stairs.

It was hot in the roof space, the heat of the sun on the tiles all day building up quite a temperature in the large room despite the fact the skylights were open.

Sewell had obviously prepared for her visit. He had gone through the stacks of painting and selected certain pictures, leaning them against the brick walls all around the room. As she stepped on to the wooden floorboards he said nothing, just beckoning her to look with a nervousness she had never seen in him before.

She toured the room, looking at each picture individually, spending some minutes studying each before moving on to the next. The subjects were all, as she might have expected from what she had seen before, studies of women. The brunette and the short-haired blonde featured in several but there were other women too, noticeably a striking and very tall brunette with hair that was so long it reached her buttocks. But whoever the models were the paintings were all, without exception, about sex, and all had the same ability to convey complex emotions as graphically as the ones Nadine had seen on her first visit. One woman, for instance, a straight-haired flaxen-coloured blonde, who featured in one painting only, was pictured naked but for a pair of white lacy

French knickers and red high heels. It was obvious from her expression that she was trying to say to the man who could only just be seen in the shadows, that she was not at all sure whether she wanted to go on, that perhaps she had made a mistake in going this far. The man's attitude was equally clear. He was not trying to cajole or persuade. He was indifferent. If she wanted to leave it didn't matter. He had no intention of begging. The man, of course, was Sewell.

Two of the pictures she had seen before had been put out but not the one of the brunette on all fours in the cream bedroom. Sewell might have thought Nadine would have been offended by its proximity to what he had done to her, the image in the mirror being too close to what she had herself experienced.

Sewell stood silently as she moved about. After she had done one circuit she started around a second time.

'I'll get the champagne,' he said, disappearing down the bare staircase.

She toured the paintings slowly. When she had been in the attic before her body had been reeling from the effects of what Sewell had done to her. Later, she had wondered whether her reaction to the paintings was conditioned by her own highly susceptible state of mind. Tonight she felt she could be more objective. It was clear Sewell had an enormous talent. His ability to convey emotion was exceptional. Why he was obsessed with the act of sex she did not know but the faces of the women he painted appeared to have a great deal more significance than the confines of what they were doing. They spoke of the human condition. He was using sex as a metaphor for life.

'I'd like to paint you,' he said quietly.

Despite the bare floorboards on the stairs she had not heard him come back and started at the sound of his voice. He had the two champagne flutes in one hand and the bottle in the other. It was dripping water on to the floor from where it had been in ice. He handed her a glass and put the champagne bottle on the table by the easel where most of his paints were stored.

'How do you do it?' she said.

'Do what?'

'Do you work with models?' That sounded as though she was asking about the models, which was not what she'd intended. 'I mean, like a life class.'

'I work from photographs.'

'Photographs.'

'Yes.' He sipped the wine. Nadine took a large swig of hers. 'You're not shocked?'

'No.'

'What then?'

She searched for the right words wanting to be accurate. 'I think they're very powerful. Affecting. They're real people.'

'Then you understand. I'm very glad.'

'They're moving.'

'Would you let me paint you?'

'Like this?' It came out rather crassly.

'Yes.'

'From photographs?'

'You're a beautiful woman, Nadine. I've been thinking about you.'

He took one step towards her and held out his hand. It was wet from the champagne bottle. She looked at it and then up into his eyes. She had been looking at his eyes in the pictures. Ten different expressions. Expressions of passion, lust, interest, indifference, exhilaration. But in none of the pictures had she seen what she could see so clearly now, an expression of adoration. It made her feel weak. Her resolve, her determination, her game plan, drained away like rain down a gutter. She felt as she had that first night.

He picked up her hand. His fingers were cold from the bottle. He touched her fingertips to his lips without taking his eyes from hers.

Without a word he pulled her towards the stairs. The next thing she knew she was standing in the cream bedroom, unable to remember how she had got there, and he was taking the glass from her hand, putting it beside his on the bedside table. He wrapped his arms around her and kissed her full on the mouth, his hard body pressing into her as his arms hugged her fiercely. She felt his cock unfurling against her stomach.

'No,' she said once, breaking her lips away from his only to have them captured again. She felt her own needs and desires swamping her resistance, her body asserting itself so strongly she throbbed with a wave of sensation that was rooted in her sex. 'No, no, no, no . . .' she heard herself saying somewhere in her mind though she said nothing. It was useless to resist. She was out of control.

He pressed forward, pushing his erection into her belly. They were standing by the double bed, the back of her legs pushing against the mattress. She felt herself falling backward, literally and metaphorically. He fell on top of her, their arms and legs tangled together, their mouths still joined.

But as he tried to roll her into the centre of the bed she resisted. She may have lost her way emotionally but sexually she knew what she wanted and was determined to get it. She wriggled free from his grasp and sat up.

He appeared unperturbed. He didn't see this as a rejection. He was too arrogant for that and had too much insight into what she was feeling – the insight he used in his work. Would this moment be frozen in time on one of his canvasses? Is that why they were all so powerful, because of the emotion he provoked in women? Nadine realised it was impossible to divorce her feelings about him from her feelings about his paintings.

His work made her feel the same things she had felt about him the first time they'd met. It was stunning, brilliant, extraordinary. She was turned on by it, not only because of its subject matter, though that too, but because of its raw energy and power. Just as she was turned on by the raw energy and power of Sewell himself.

She knew all her carefully planned strategies and resolutions had been abandoned but she didn't care. She didn't want to think about that. She didn't want to *think* about anything.

Nadine began unbuttoning his shirt. He lay back without interfering. She avoided looking into his eyes. When she had done with his shirt, she undid the button on the front of his jeans and unzipped his fly. She could feel his erection underneath. Parting the trousers she fished inside. His penis sprung up from the opening in his boxer shorts, glad to be free of its constriction.

Without any hesitation, she plunged her mouth onto his cock, sucking it in so hard she heard him gasp. She didn't care if she hurt him. Not now. Not like this. Not now he'd made her break her promises to herself.

She felt his cock throb as her tongue flicked against his phallus. He was so hard. She had never known a man so hard. It was as if his cock was made from stone. Except it was not cold like stone. It was hot. She sucked him again.

Pulling away, she looked down at him.

'Is that what you want?'

'Of course,' he said. 'But it's not *all* I want.'

A new emotion had gathered in Nadine, like grey storm clouds in a yellow sky. It started as resentment, resentment that he was making her behave like this, resentment at her lack of control. Soon, resentment became anger. She was angry with him for what he was making her feel.

'What else?' she said, scrambling off the bed. She could have walked straight out of the bedroom and out of the house but she was completely incapable of doing that.

She reached behind her back and pulled down the

zip of the dress. The nylon jaws sung as they parted. She pushed the shoulder straps off and wriggled the dress down over her hips.

Nadine watched his eyes, wanting to see his surprise. She wasn't wearing a bra. Her high round breasts quivered as she finally pulled free of the dress.

'Is this what you want?'

She had chosen a wide black lace suspender belt and dark black stockings. That was all. She wasn't wearing any panties.

'Yes,' he said firmly. 'I'd like to paint you like that.'

'But not fuck me?' She wanted to be crude. She stood with her legs apart and her arms akimbo. She was making a statement. His pictures spoke for him. This spoke for her. She had been foolish. He had made her feel foolish. He existed on a different plane. He was not concerned with bourgeois morality. His paintings were about sex, about life, about what mattered, not about social niceties and schoolgirl neuroses. *This* was what mattered.

He got up from the bed and quickly pulled his clothes off.

'How did you know?'

'Know what?'

'That I would find this so exciting?'

'Don't all men?' There was a little triumph in that. He wasn't a god after all. He was just another man who lusted after women in black stockings.

'Do they?'

'Oh yes.'

'I haven't seen any for a long time.'

It sounded as though it were true but it was hard to believe. A trickle of fluid was running down from the slit of his urethra. He sat on the edge of the bed.

'Couldn't you get one of your models to oblige?'

'I just didn't think of it.' His face looked as though he was trying to work out why, as though he were wrestling with an aesthetic problem. 'You will let me paint you, won't you?'

'I don't want to talk about that now.'

She didn't want to talk at all. She moved one hand down to her belly. Like a glass of red wine knocked over a white tablecloth, her anger seemed to have spilled over and lay all around. She stroked the short soft hair of her pubis, stroking it in one direction, towards the apex of her thighs. She used her other hand to cup her breast. She squeezed it hard, the pliant flesh escaping between her fingers.

She was raging within herself, rebuking herself for being such a push-over while, at the same time, she was almost weeping with the emotional impact of what he made her feel. She was cross and resentful at the same time as she was overwhelmed by him, wanting him more than she had ever wanted any man. Her feelings were boiling over.

Nadine moved a finger down between her legs, pushed it between her labia and felt for her clitoris. It was already swollen. Gently she nudged it to one side and a shock of pleasure jolted through her. She looked straight at Sewell.

'Do you like doing that?' His eyes were watching the way her finger moved.

'Yes . . .'

89

'Do you do it often?'

'All the time,' she lied.

'Does it make you come?'

'I'm very good at it.'

'I can see that.'

'Do you want me to come?'

'Yes. Very much.' It was as though someone had offered him the vista of a beautiful sunset. She had a strange feeling he was watching her with an artist's eye, judging the shapes and colours and perspectives, as well as seeing her more venally. She didn't know which way she wanted to appeal to him most.

She walked around the bed to the other side. She lay on the oatmeal-coloured counterpane and opened her legs wide, bending her knee. She hadn't taken off her shoes and they dug into the material, rucking it up around the spiky heels. The side of her ankle brushed against his naked back.

Nadine felt a surge of sensation as she saw Sewell turn and look down at her. His eyes examined her minutely from her face to her ankles, then back up again, over the tight black nylon that clung to every contour of her legs, over her thigh where the nylon welt of the stocking was the darkest black and her flesh broad and full, the welt drawn into chevrons by the taut black suspender. He seemed to be fascinated by the two different colours and textures there, the harsh woven grid of nylon against the smooth silky flesh, the dark black against the creamy white. Nadine suddenly remembered what he had done to her tights that first night. For some reason she had forgotten that. Forgotten it completely.

His eyes lighted on her sex. Nadine knew it would be glistening with the sap that had leaked from her body.

Sewell got up and knelt on the bed at the side of her hip. He made no attempt to touch her. She could see his cock was leaking a sticky viscous fluid.

She buried the fingers of her right hand in her sex again and felt the little nut of her clitoris react immediately, pulsing wildly. Her body was firmly in control now, its needs established, any thought of what she should and should not be doing banished totally. She wanted to show him, wanted him to see exactly what it was like for her. She wanted to show him *her* sexual emotions as he'd shown her those of the other women in his pictures. She needed him to know she was special too.

'Watch me,' she said unnecessarily.

Her orgasm had already begun. She recognised the tell-tale signs. She had never behaved like this with any man, never dressed so blatantly for sex, never been so wanton, never allowed a man to see her do what she was doing now. The fact that she was doing it for Sewell excited her as much as any physical contact. Which was not to say she didn't want the pressure of her fingertip moving with absolute regularity against her clitoris.

She arched her body off the bed, digging her heels into the bedding and supporting her weight on her shoulders. Awkwardly, twisting her body to reach, she snaked her other hand under her thigh, until she could feel her fingers at the entrance of her sex. Using two fingers she pushed into the opening, then

91

scissored her fingers apart stretching the elastic flesh as if wanting to show him how supple it was. Then she pushed her fingers deep and felt her sex closing around them. She had never felt herself so hot or so wet. More than that, the silky soft flesh that lined her sex seemed to have become as sensitive as the nerves of her clitoris.

Nadine listened to the rhythms of her body, the pulse that throbbed harder and stronger by the minute. It was taking her over, concentrating the world on the tiny space between her legs. She looked down at herself, her stockinged legs bent, the suspenders at the front not taut now but looped upward, the suspenders at the side still stretched, cutting into the spongy flesh of her hip. She saw her breasts trembling and her nipples pucker, the ring of tan brown areola that surrounded them pimpled with excitement.

The rhythms became more insistent, a hammering that echoed in her ear drums. At every fifth or sixth beat the intensity increased and she felt a surge of feeling that made her gasp, her mouth open, her head tossing from side to side. She plunged the fingers of her left hand into her sex and out again, imitating the action of a cock, straining the tendons of her hand to force them deeper. This was new for her. Until she had bought the dildo her masturbation ritual had never involved penetration. She had contented herself with stimulating her clitoris, prodding and pushing and circling it. But she found she needed penetration too and the inner contours of her body became new territory to explore, giving her extra stimulation.

It excited him too, of course. So she performed for him, put on a show. She wanted to show him her body in extremis.

The buffeting her body was taking, like a small boat on a stormy sea, was getting greater by the minute, the waves of feeling almost overwhelming her. She turned her head to look into his eyes. The expression on his face looked distant and glazed as though he were seeing another reality. She had the impression he was seeing her in a picture, imagining how he would paint her, how he would bring to life the emotion that was written in every line of her body. Strangely the idea made her even more excited. She squirmed down on her hands, wriggling her hips but still staring up at him.

She was so close now, her orgasm held back by the slenderest of threads, that she pulled her hands away from her sex. The wave of sensation that would break the thread was already in her body and she wanted him to be able to see her sex: open, wanton, displayed. To see what she was capable of. She wanted this to be the picture he painted.

But he had other ideas. With his considerable strength he took her by the arm and rolled her over onto her stomach. In an instant before she had time to react, he had fallen on her, his muscular body covering hers, his hard, strong cock forcing its way into the cleft of her buttocks.

'This is what *I* want,' he hissed into her ear.

His glans was pressing into the crater of her anus. The copious juices her masturbation had produced had run out of her labia and the corrugated flesh of her rear hole was wet – wet enough to let him push into her.

'No,' she said involuntarily, her whole body going rigid as she felt the hardness of his cock inch up into her rear. The ring of muscles there knitted together to form an impenetrable barrier.

'Please,' he said.

She wanted to, she wanted it badly. Her body was boiling with excitement. She wanted to give him this, show him there were no limits, show him she was prepared to do anything for him.

But her body had other ideas. With a deliberate act of concentration she tried to relax. The tension in her legs and arms disappeared. She relaxed her belly and tried to breath more normally but the muscles against which she could feel his phallus were locked and nothing she could do would release them.

She felt him pushing forward but he made no impression. Far from effecting entry the movement only served to hurt her. She felt her muscles spasm, their rigidity increased.

'I want to,' she said.

'No.'

With balletic ease he rolled off her, turned her onto her back and fell on her again, his cock powering into her in one fluid movement, so that one second she was open and empty and the next she was so full of him it felt as though she might burst. The pain and tension between her buttocks was wiped away as if it had never existed. He didn't attempt to move back and forth. He just held himself deep inside her, so deep his glans pressed against the neck of her womb, every muscle of his body concentrated on that connection.

The move he had made had been so sudden and so powerful that Nadine hardly had time to feel the heat of his cock inside her before her orgasm broke loose. It ripped through her body with a force so great it carried her into another dimension, a dimension where there was only sensation, where seas of pleasure threw great waves onto the shores of her senses, crashing down one after the other, rivalling each other in intensity. Flashbulbs exploded in her head illuminating nothing but scarlet and crimson joy.

Her body shuddered over and over again. Her hands clutched at his back, her fingers like claws trying to grip his flesh, seeking support as her orgasm renewed itself endlessly.

Finally, her body began to relax and she felt him start to move. She remembered how he had felt last time, his whole body as adamantine as his cock. It was as though his whole body was a phallus, a phallus she could put her arms around and hold.

His penis slid back and forth lubricated by her juices. It filled her completely, physically and mentally. There was not a niche of her sex that wasn't occupied by it, not a part of her mind that thought of anything else. Every sinew of tissue was stretched to accommodate him. She couldn't remember him feeling this big last time.

Her mind was playing tricks with her. She hadn't remembered the way he ground the base of his shaft against her clitoris either, grinding it from side to side so the little nut was trapped between her pubic bone and his cock, between a rock and a hard place, making it throb anew.

Time had simply ceased to exist. In seconds, or was it hours, her orgasm came around again like a summer storm. She could feel the distant thunder and the sparks of lightning getting closer. The surges of feeling became stronger, the echoes of one thunderclap superimposed on the stirrings of the next.

He was relentless. He did nothing else but power his cock into her, driving it forward as far as he could, then pulling it out again until his glans was poised at the outer rim, kissed by her labia, before plunging in again. The forward stroke took her breath away.

She clung to him. She moved her hands down to his buttocks so she could feel the muscles that drove his cock into her. He was making her come again, the storm approaching rapidly now. It was as though her first orgasm, for all its force, was only the prelude to this one, the strength of the tempest surging through her nerves. She dug her fingers into his buttocks, urging him on, knowing he could go no deeper, but wanting him deeper nevertheless.

Nadine would never know whether it was timed deliberately or whether it was purely accidental but it was at that moment that Betty Holden opened the bedroom door and walked in.

'What a pretty picture.'

Chapter Four

'What a pretty picture.'

Nadine snapped her head to the side to look at the petite brunette who was walking over to the bed, her eyes on Sewell's buttocks as they rose and fell with the regularity of a metronome. Nadine was too far gone to protest. The brunette's level stare had only one result. It turned Nadine on. She felt her body seethe.

Calmly Betty sat on the side of the bed and stroked her hand over Sewell's buttocks and Nadine's hand.

'He's so good at it, isn't he?' she said quietly, as matter-of-factly as if she were talking about the weather.

Nadine could not answer and had no need to. Her whole body was locked in a paroxysm of pleasure so extreme it was rigid. Her mouth opened to try and make a sound but nothing came out. What was happening to her? Instead of pushing Sewell off and confronting this woman, whoever she was, she was enjoying it. She relished the thought that this stranger could see Sewell's cock burrowing into her, pitching her into an orgasm that made her cry out loud and long as it seized her body.

A thousand questions swam into her mind but none of them mattered. It was as if her mind was in a separate compartment, so far away from what was happening to her it might have been another place and time altogether. All that mattered was her excitement.

She knew the woman immediately. Though she had never seen her before in her life she knew her intimately. She had seen her in precisely the parlous state she was in now, ecstasy etched on her face, Sewell's sex buried inside her. She was unmistakably the brunette in the pictures in the attic.

The memory of one particular picture, of this woman on her knees on the bed looking into the mirror, brought a frisson of such pleasure to Nadine it fed into her orgasm, wringing another shock of sensation out of her.

She looked straight into the brunette's eyes as she clung to Sewell's body and his cock pummelled into her regardless. He was so strong, so big, so hot. The brunette's expression was changing. From quizzical interest her eyes began to dance with the flames of excitement. Her passion fuelled Nadine's.

An odd thing happened. Just as she'd wanted to show herself to Sewell, now with equal fervour she wanted to show the brunette what she was feeling. It was an odd *quid pro quo*, as if in some strange way she owed it to the other woman for what she had shown of herself in the painting.

'I'm coming again,' she said, wanting the brunette to know. It was true. The circle of her latest orgasm had been completed only to start another.

'I know,' the woman said softly, smiling, her hand pressing Nadine's fingers into Sewell's buttocks.

This time there was no slow build-up. Nadine's

orgasm simply exploded. It was not only her body that was overloaded with sensation but her mind. She was so astonished at her own reactions and so many images were rushing through her head – Sewell's body on hers, the painting in the attic, the look in the brunette's eyes – that it was simply impossible to sort one from another. Impossible to think at all. All she could do was respond, surrendering to the sensations that picked her up like the hand of a giant and wrung her out remorselessly until there was nothing left. At last her nerves were drained and her body, for its own protection, shut down all sensation. Suddenly she found herself floating free, dissociated from immediate realities.

She had not lost consciousness but, as her crisis passed, it felt as if she was waking from a dream. The orgasm had forced her eyes closed but she was in no hurry to open them again. She embraced the blackness as a way of seeking anonymity, wanting time to think now that thought was possible again, to work out her reactions. She felt Sewell roll off her, his erection sliding from her sex, its final departure causing a spasm in her body that made her gasp.

No other man had ever aroused such emotions in her. When she had walked into the house she had planned exactly what she would do. That plan had simply been shunted aside. Her reactions, to him and to his paintings – or was that the same thing? – had made her feel nothing but a passionate need for him. Her lust had overwhelmed every other priority, the need for an explanation of what she had found in this bedroom on her last visit had been forgotten or, at least, overtaken by events.

Now the explanation was sitting on the bed beside her looking down at her semi-naked body, the body she had dressed so deliberately for Sewell. She tried to work out what her reaction should be but her mind could not come up with one. Every attitude she might strike would have implications and consequences she could not fathom out. She had only one priority now, completely the reverse of what she had calculated so carefully before she arrived; she didn't want to lose Sewell.

That didn't mean she was not entitled to an explanation.

The silence in the room was becoming oppressive.

She opened her eyes and sat up. Her heart was beating fast.

'Who is this?' she asked quietly.

'She lives here, some of the time.'

'Her nightdress.' That was not a question. 'Why did you hide it from me?'

'I thought you might find the idea objectionable and I very much wanted to take you to bed.'

'And you don't mind?' She looked at the brunette trying to be calm and keep the astonishment out of her voice.

'My name's Betty. And you're Nadine. He's told me about you.' She smiled a knowing smile, complicity in a world Nadine did not understand.

'You don't mind?' she repeated.

'Why should I mind. Sewell's Sewell. Besides . . .' The brunette got to her feet. '. . . I like it.'

She was wearing a red cocktail dress in a satiny silk. It had long sleeves and a polo neck and fitted tightly over her very full chest and narrow waist, around which a wide red leather belt was cinched. Her shapely but short legs were bare and very tanned and she wore very high heels in red suede. She unzipped the dress at the side, removed the belt, and peeled the dress off.

'What are you doing?' Nadine said.

'She's getting undressed,' Sewell said calmly.

The brunette was wearing a tight black body under the dress, its plunging neckline revealing a great deal of the large bosom Nadine had seen in the paintings.

'Aren't you even going to say you're sorry?' Nadine asked, then wished she hadn't.

'Sorry for what? Sorry for making you come? Sorry for giving you better sex than you've ever had in your life?'

'Don't be so arrogant,' Nadine snapped angrily, furious because his knowledge of her was too close to the truth.

'Nadine, I told you. Please don't let's get into some bourgeois scene. This is how I live. If you don't like it, just leave. It's as simple as that. You've got your explanation. I *am* sorry it came out this way. But things got out of hand. I was going to explain it to you downstairs but I wanted you to see the pictures. I hoped you'd see something in them, see what I need . . . I didn't mean for Betty just to barge in.'

'I'm used to it,' said Betty. She was pulling the straps of the black body off her shoulders and, without the slightest self-consciousness, stripped it off her breasts. They were as big and pendulous as the paintings had suggested. Her nipples were big too, a deep ruby red.

'Used to what?'

'I told you, Nadine, Sewell is Sewell. You just have to accept it. He wants to paint you, did he tell you that?'

'Yes.'

'And you've seen the pictures so you must have known.'

'Known what?' Almost as she said it, the penny dropped. The majority of the pictures in the attic had been with Sewell and two other women. She had thought about it at the time but had decided it was some sort of artistic conceit, not a reality.

Betty shrugged as though further explanation was unnecessary. She slipped the black body down over her hips and let it fall to the floor. She stepped out of the garment, stooping to pick it up, then threw it over her dress which she had left on the bedroom chair. Her black pubic hair was thick and bushy.

Sewell got to his feet, his erection still as hard as it had been earlier, and came up behind Betty. He kissed her neck, wrapping his arms around her and cupping her big breasts in his hands. His eyes were looking straight at Nadine, their full force turned on her, transmitting the power and strength of his personality.

'I hope you'll stay,' he said.

'Stay?'

'Stay with me. Stay with us. Be with us.'

Nadine felt as though she had stepped in quicksand. The harder she tried to understand, the more she sank into the mire. The situation was so unlike anything she had ever been confronted with before she found it impossible to work out what she wanted to do.

'I think I should go home,' she said hesitantly. She got off the bed.

'You're running away,' Sewell said, his voice strong and clear. 'Just be sure you know what you're running away from. It's not your own needs. I can see what you want Nadine. You're going because that's what you think you should do, not because of what you want.'

'I'm not running away.'

'What are you afraid of?'

Betty slipped out of Sewell's arms and slid gracefully to her knees right in front of Nadine. Her hands curled around Nadine's buttocks and she levered her face into Nadine's soft fleecy pubis. As if guided by some homing signal, her tongue inched between Nadine's wet labia straight onto her clit.

'God . . .' It was a cry of surprise not at Betty's actions but at the shock of pleasure they produced in Nadine's body. Instantly she felt herself melting, melting over the hot wet tongue that manipulated her clitoris so artfully. The desire to push Betty away, to react indignantly was crushed almost before it was conceived.

She had never thought about sex with women, never imagined what it would be like with one, never even in her wildest dreams. She would have imagined her reaction to Betty's assault would have been horror, followed by revulsion. But it was not. Perhaps it would have been before she met Sewell. Now she felt nothing of the kind. Instead, to her astonishment, she felt an entirely different emotion. For the first time in her life she felt desire for the body of another woman. Sexual desire, a desire to hold and touch and kiss her, desire as strong as any she'd felt for a man. She saw herself pressed against the brunette's naked body, feeling those heavy breasts, pushing her thigh into the woman's naked crotch and feeling her sex, hot and wet. The thoughts tumbled into her mind as though they had been behind some hidden wall that had suddenly started to crumble away. She saw herself kissing her, plunging her tongue into her small delicate mouth. She saw herself down between her legs, dipping her head to her nether lips.

She shuddered. Betty felt it. She worked her tongue against the lozenge of Nadine's clitoris, feeling it pulsing like a tiny penis.

Sewell came around behind Nadine. He pressed his erection into the cleft of her buttocks and wrapped his arms around her, cupping her breasts just as he had with Betty.

'Go if you want to,' he whispered.

'It's too late,' she whispered back. Did the words carry an implication of regret? Was she lost beyond recall? Or were they a realisation that, in the short time it had taken for her body to become aware of a core of undreamt-of pleasure, her life had changed dramatically and irrevocably? She did not know and, at this moment, she did not care. There would be time for regret later. At the moment she wanted to be with Sewell and with Betty. She wanted it all.

Betty pulled her head back, smiled up at Nadine and got to her feet. She walked over to the bed, pulled off the counterpane and the top sheet and lay down on her back, her breasts hanging down on either side of her chest, like over-ripe fruit.

'Come on,' she urged quietly. 'Come to me . . .'

Sewell's hands dropped from Nadine's body, freeing her. As though in a trance Nadine walked over to the bed. She sat down on the edge of it and turned to look at Betty's naked body. She saw her own hand, as though it belonged to someone else, reaching out to stroke Betty's thigh. Even this small act was a major step for Nadine. She had never touched a woman like this, like she would have touched a man, stroking her hand up and down in order to arouse. Betty's skin felt impossibly soft and creamy, the flesh yielding and pliant. Nadine's fingers brushed Betty's wiry black pubic hair.

'I can't do it,' she said but as she heard the words she knew it wasn't true.

Betty opened her legs slightly, not wide enough to let Nadine see her sex but enough to give her a view of the top of her labia and the furrow that ran between them. Nadine stared at it and, at the same time, saw herself staring, as though she was watching the whole scene from a vantage point high above the bed.

She watched her hand moving up Betty's body to gather her breast in her hand, weighing it, then pinching the large ruby-red nipple. She watched herself lean forward and feed the nipple into her mouth, sucking on it, biting it lightly with her teeth, and feeling its corrugated stiffness. She watched herself kneeling up on the bed, and prying Betty's thighs apart with her hands, wide apart so her sex was revealed, her labia thick and rubbery, covered with a forest of black hair. She watched herself crawling between Betty's legs and wrapping her hands under Betty's buttocks as she dipped her head down to her sex. All this as if it were happening to someone else.

But as she pressed her lips against Betty's labia, as for the first time in her life she felt a woman's sex against her mouth and used her tongue to slip between the smooth nether lips to find Betty's clitoris – as many men had done to her – she was shocked out of her detachment by a jolt of pure, raw excitement. She squirmed her lips against Betty's sex. It was like a mouth, a vertical mouth, and she kissed it like one, feeling her own sex throbbing.

It had all happened so quickly she hadn't had time to think about it. She had never imagined what it would be like to make love to another woman but, as she pressed herself into the heat and wetness and incredible softness of another woman's sex, she felt sensations so strong that she knew it must have been part of her for a long time, like a secret compartment of her psyche now suddenly revealed. Surely that could be the only explanation for feelings so strong?

She felt a rush, like the floodgates opening. Suddenly she wanted everything at once. Her tongue found Betty's clitoris. It was large and engorged. She manipulated it the way she loved men to do with her, pushing it from side to side then up and down, pressing it hard against the pubic bone beneath. Betty gasped loudly.

'That's so good,' she said as if Nadine needed reassurance.

Nadine wanted more. She pushed the fingers of one hand under Betty's thigh until they were nestling in her labia. Without any hesitation she found the entrance to Betty's vagina and pushed two, then three, fingers inside. It was the same hand that she had used earlier on her own sex but the sensation was quite different. She felt Betty's sex contract around the invaders as though sucking them in. She pushed deeper, as deep as her fingers would go, stretching against the tendons of her hand. There seemed to be a pulse in there, a strong throbbing pulse. It matched exactly the feeling Nadine's own body was generating.

'And you . . .' It was Sewell's voice. His hands were on her hips. He lifted her bodily over Betty's thigh and around, until her legs were alongside Betty's head and all she had to do was swing her thigh over Betty's shoulders. She did not hesitate. She hadn't lost contact with Betty's sex while Sewell had moved her, though her fingers had been pulled clear. Now, as she raised her thigh and poised herself above Betty's mouth, she redoubled her efforts, plunging her fingers home again and squirming her mouth harder again the rubbery labia, while her tongue pressed into the clitoris.

She felt Betty's hands snake around her thighs, over the welts of the black stockings, pulling her open sex down onto her mouth with a firm insistent pressure. Betty's head came up off the sheet to meet it and the artful tongue Nadine had already felt immediately nuzzled into her clitoris again.

It was the completion of a circle of sensation unlike anything Nadine had ever felt. As she used her tongue to lick and nudge against the swollen nut of Betty's clitoris, Betty's tongue did the same to her. As her fingers played in Betty's sex, Betty's fingers parted her labia to penetrate hers. Every action provoked a similar reaction, every feeling was reciprocated, every sensation exchanged. The circle was so perfect, so complete, that Nadine could feel everything Betty was feeling. She could feel the exact moment when the brunette's body began to change from merely enjoying the sensations of pleasure to a more urgent need, like a car slipping into a high gear, because that was precisely what was happening to her. As the nerves in her body began to knit together, a common chorus of exhilaration singing rhythmically in each one, she felt Betty's body pounding too at the same tempo and the same increasing urgency.

The circle of pleasure was amplified. Every touch, every throbbing pulse, every sensation seemed to be doubled. Their bodies squirmed against each other, Betty's breasts squashed out to the side, Nadine's nipples pressed hard against Betty's silky stomach.

They were coming together because it would have been impossible not to. The explosion of sensation in one was indistinguishable from the explosion in the other. They had created a writhing hydra of exquisite pleasure. They clung to each other, fighting for breath, no longer able to do anything but feel, their bodies locked and rigid, Nadine's mind blanked out by passion.

As the tide of sensation ebbed and their muscles thawed from rigidity, Nadine rolled off Betty's body. She was actually tingling, her nerves' reaction to the most intense orgasms she had ever experienced. Her mind was affected too. She found it difficult to think, to form an idea, to do anything but register what was happening to her.

She looked at Sewell. He was sitting on the bed. He had watched everything. There was a knowing look in his eyes, a look of 'I told you so', as if he'd known all along that Nadine would react the way she had.

'I want to paint you like this,' he said. 'In the aftermath.'

'Lying beside me,' Betty added.

Sewell turned to look at Betty. He leant forward and kissed her on the mouth, her lips still wet from the juices of Nadine's body.

'Tastes good,' he whispered.

'Mmm . . .'

Betty sat up. She reached down to Sewell's lap and grasped his erection as if it were the handle of some strange machine. She squeezed it tightly in her fist.

'I know what you need now.'

She got up onto her knees, on all fours, as she'd been in the picture, the position Nadine had been in on this bed too. Her sex, the curly black hair plastered down by a mixture of Nadine's saliva and her own wetness, was facing Nadine: the mouth of her vagina was open, the labia loose and relaxed.

Sewell knelt on the bed behind her. His erection bobbed up and down and he got himself into position. When he was nestling between Betty's fleshy buttocks, his hands on her hips, he looked over his shoulder at Nadine wanting to see her reaction.

It was pretty obvious. Despite her exhaustion, she was not too tired to watch. She had never seen this, never been in a room with a couple naked and having sex, let alone this close. She shivered, the remnants of orgasm still playing in her body like background noise.

His eyes, those deep limpid pools of fathomless emotion, looked at her and through her. She could hide nothing from him, not her excitement nor her desire. He seemed to be challenging her, as he had when he first walked into her office, demanding a response – a response that went beyond anything any man had asked of her before.

'Kiss me.' He hadn't needed to say it. It was what Nadine wanted. She wanted to kiss him and she wanted him to use Betty.

Trying to ignore the tremors of sensation that still rippled from her sex she got to her knees. She came up alongside Sewell and he kissed her lightly. But Nadine wanted more. She hooked her hand around the back of his neck and pulled him onto her mouth, plunging her tongue between his lips until it came up against his.

She felt him buck his hips. His cock slid down between Betty's buttocks but not into her sex. This time Sewell didn't need to tell her what to do. While her lips played over his mouth Nadine dropped her hand down his back, delved between his legs and felt his heavy ball sac and then the base of his shaft. Beyond that, Betty's sex exuded heat.

For a moment the heat and sticky wetness down there overwhelmed Nadine. She was so sensitised now, even brushing Betty's sex accidentally as she did, produced a surge of excitement she could barely control. But she renewed her attack on Sewell's mouth as a means of concentrating and, at the same time, wrapped her fingers around his shaft, pushing it down into Betty's waiting maw.

'God . . . so hot,' Betty moaned.

It was. His cock was like a poker that had been left in the fire. First the fire of Nadine's body, then the flames of excitement as he watched the two women perform and now the almost unbearable heat of Betty's primed and pampered sex.

Nadine clung onto his balls, pulling the sac away from his body and jiggling them in her hand. He gasped, expelling hot air into her mouth, then breaking the kiss, needing air, her sucking mouth too much stimulation in combination with the nether mouth that sucked at him too. He had held back for too long.

'Yes, Sewell,' Betty said raising her head, her voice crystal clear.

Nadine was in control now. It was all up to her. Sewell wasn't moving. He had thrust himself into

111

Betty's body and was content to let Nadine's fingers, pulling and playing with his balls, propel him to orgasm, as they had done before.

'Darling,' he muttered, looking at her, his eyes burning away the layers of pretence until he could see her soul.

She pulled hard, pulled the ball sac down and felt his cock jerk immediately. She wanted to show him she wasn't totally naive, she wasn't just some hapless innocent, a fly that had fallen into his web. She wanted to show him she wasn't frightened, that what had happened had occurred because she had wanted it to, and not because she had been seduced or had fallen into any sexual trap that he and Betty had devised.

He was looking at her still, reading the expressions that flitted across her face: excitement, defiance, pride.

She released his ball sac and circled the base of his cock with her fingers. It was slippery and wet from Betty's juices. She squeezed it hard, feeling Betty's labia at the side of her fingers.

She saw the look of surprise in his face and then almost immediately saw his eyes roll up. At the same moment, she felt his cock jerk, spasming inside the tight confines of Betty's sex, his muscular body rigid as he came at long last, the waiting making the final spending seem to go on forever.

His dying thrusts took Betty over the edge. She lifted her head and looked into the mirror, fighting to keep her eyes open.

Nadine looked into the mirror too. She could see

their three faces framed together in the glass, Betty's ecstasy all too apparent. It was a moment crystallised in time, like a photograph. Suddenly she realised it was the situation depicted exactly in Sewell's painting, the one that had fascinated her most – the brunette on her knees, the dark-eyed man behind her, the blonde with short hair alongside them. She was the blonde.

'I want to paint you.' It was the first thing Sewell said as he opened his eyes.

The phone on her desk rang once. Nadine picked it up.

'It's John Sewell,' her secretary said.

'Tell him I'm still busy.'

'It's the third time he's called.'

'Tell him I'm out at a meeting.'

'I did. He doesn't believe me.'

'Dawn, I don't care what you tell him. Just get rid of him. I'm not going to talk to him.'

'If you say so.'

'I do,' Nadine said putting the phone down.

She got up from her desk and saw Dawn talking into the phone on the other side of the glass partition. It was unlike Sewell to be so persistent. The first time he had taken rejection without demure. This time he had called three times in two hours. But Nadine was not curious as to what he wanted to say. She absolutely did not want to speak to him.

She paced the room, going over to the window to stare out at the view of the rooftops of London and the Post Office Tower to the north, but saw nothing.

She picked up the brief of the presentation she was making this afternoon and sat in the leather armchair on the other side of the desk to review it. As she opened its cover she noticed her hand was trembling. It was the mention of Sewell's name that had done that.

She tried to focus on the pages in front of her — the presentation to the manufacturer of a supposedly revolutionary sanitary towel. The brightly coloured graphics and columns of figures depicted estimated sales growth and revealed how the advertising spend was to be distributed over various media, together with all the other details the client would need to know. Nadine found she could only see a blur of print.

'Dawn,' she shouted through to her secretary. 'Coffee, please.'

She managed to read through the first couple of pages but found her mind drifting. She had been a coward last night. The cold fingers of regret had closed around her heart and mind so rapidly, as she lay on one side of Sewell, with Betty on the other, that she had not been able to sleep. Nor did she want to face either of them in the morning. Moving as quietly as she could, she'd gathered up her clothes and crept, like a thief in the night, out of the house.

But leaving like that had left the situation unresolved. Had she stayed to face Sewell in the cold light of day with Betty lying next to him, her voluptuous body naked and provoking, she would have been able to sort out her own feelings. But in running away she had run away from the truth and now she wasn't at all sure what the truth was.

She could not deny her sexual pleasure and the extremities to which Sewell, and then Betty, had driven her. But how she was going to cope with the knowledge that her first experience with a woman had been so markedly exciting, was an entirely different matter. Had she hidden from herself for years a secret longing to have sex with a woman? Or was it Sewell's magnetism, his enormous sexual energy that had somehow overwhelmed her and taken her into realms of experience she would never have contemplated on her own?

Whatever it was, she knew she did not want to repeat the experiment. Of that she had been quite certain from the moment she had slipped back into her dress in the hallway of Sewell's house and crept down his stairs. She had frightened herself badly, like a child wandering too far from home. And, like a child, she wanted to run back to the confines of her safe, ordered and comfortable life, slamming the door firmly on what had scared her so much.

'Coffee.' The voice made her start. It was Barbara Geddes. 'I caught Dawn on the way in with it.'

'Hi, Barbara.' Nadine was glad to see her friend.

Barbara set two cups on the white coffee table in front of Nadine's chair and slumped onto the small leather sofa of the same design. Her big body made it look even smaller.

'You look rough.'

'Thanks.'

'There's no doubt about what you got up to last night.'

'Isn't there?' Nadine tried to pretend innocence.

'Who was it, then? Someone new?'

'Sewell,' Nadine confessed.

'Sewell? I thought he'd been given the big E.'

'He had. He has. I should never have gone back.'

'Looks as though he gave you a good time.'

Nadine lent forward in the chair and sipped at the coffee. 'He did.' She contemplated telling Barbara the whole story but then decided not to. Perhaps she would eventually but the wound was still open and Barbara's directness would not help the scar tissue to form.

'So?'

'It's no good, Barbara. He's involved with someone else. Heavily involved.'

'But not married?'

'What difference does that make?'

'You could muscle in.'

'I don't want to. I really don't want to. Not after last night.'

'Sounds intriguing. What did he want to do? Put on your underwear?'

'Stop it. I'm hurt. I hurt myself. I should never have gone to see him again. It was playing with fire.'

'Fire. Wow! I haven't been near a real fire for months. Sounds like fun.'

Nadine suddenly saw Sewell and Barbara together, Barbara on all fours on the bed, Sewell behind her. She saw herself too, her hand moving down his back . . . she shuddered.

'I'll tell you the whole story one day.'

'Can't wait. Listen, I came in to talk about the Pantie-Pad presentation but, before I forget, are you free next Wednesday for dinner?'

'Hold on.' Nadine consulted the diary on her desk. The days were crammed with appointments but the evenings were depressingly free. 'Is this one of your blind dates?'

'Certainly not,' Barbara lied.

'Wednesday's fine,' she said writing 'Barbara' in capitals on the appropriate page. 'What's the matter with us? Two gorgeous, sexy women and not a man in sight.'

'Two gorgeous career-orientated women. That's the difference.'

'Is it?'

'Of course. Are you going to sit around at home all day listening to Woman's Hour on the radio, cooking *pot-au-feu* and making wholemeal bread, waiting for the sound of hubby's key in the front door? Of course you're not.'

'Is that what men want?'

'They think they want this.' She gestured at their smart business suits, nylon-sheathed legs and trim high heels. 'They think they want lovely elegantly dressed women who look a million dollars in a lacy black teddy. But in the end they want someone who puts their meal on the table and produces something cuddly for them to play with after work and at weekends.'

'And as soon as they get that they yearn for the sexy woman in the black lace teddy again?'

'Exactly. That's life, isn't it? We all yearn for what we haven't got.'

'So what's this dinner in aid of?'

'Just some friends.' Barbara had a mischievous look in her eyes. She was up to something but at that moment Nadine did not have the energy to ask her what it was.

'We'd better go over the Pantie-Pad presentation.'

'The great debate – wings or no wings?'

'Wings. These have got great big wings. The biggest wings yet. I'd have suggested they used elephants ears in the commercial but they wouldn't have been amused.'

'Is there a press angle?'

'New product, new ideas.'

'Old idea, revamped product and a company that's making more money out of selling sanitary towels to women than Dr White would ever have believed possible.'

Nadine laughed. It was the first time she had laughed that day.

She locked the door with a big brass key. He was waiting for her. She couldn't see him properly but she knew he was there. He was sitting with a glass of champagne in his hand on a Victorian saloon chair, the champagne bottle on a round mahogany wine table. He was wearing a thick velvet robe the colour of burgundy and she knew he was quite naked underneath.

She stood on a little circular rostrum a foot high that was just big enough to accommodate a plain upright chair. The darkness in the rest of the room was emphasised by the intensity of the light that illuminated the rostrum, so much light that it warmed her skin.

She had dressed specially for this. She had put on her make-up carefully, using dark heavy colours and thick lipstick painted on with a brush. Her eyes were shadowed and outlined dramatically, with blusher on her cheeks that made them look hollow and deep red nail varnish on her fingers and toes. She had wanted to look like a whore, a very expensive, very exclusive whore, but a whore nonetheless.

She had chosen her clothes for the same reason. Her blouse was tight, with a plunging neckline that revealed the cleavage of her breasts, her skirt was split almost to the top of her thigh and her shoes were black patent leather with heels so high she felt she was walking on tip-toe.

'Go on.' His voice thrilled her. It was as thick as the velvet of his robe.

She unzipped her skirt at the side and let it fall, turning her back on him so he would see her buttocks emerge first.

'That's what you wanted, isn't it?' she said.

Stepping out of the skirt, she kicked it aside with her foot and quickly unbuttoned her blouse. She stripped it off and stood arms akimbo so he could look at what she had chosen for him. She was wearing a tight black basque, boned and waisted, made from silk and lace. It hugged her body, its bra pushing her breasts up and out, its long suspenders holding her sheer black stockings taut. She wasn't wearing any panties. She didn't wear panties with him.

Satisfied that he had seen enough of this pose, she turned her back on him again and bent over, opening her legs wide and grasping her ankles with her hands. She knew he would be looking into her sex, knew her vulva would be open and exposed, the bright light searching out every detail. She knew it was framed by the long black suspenders along the sides of her thighs and the welts of the black stockings across them. She knew it would glisten too because she could feel her excitement.

But she wanted to show him more. She wanted to be a whore for him. That's what he wanted, wasn't it?

Without straightening up she slid her right hand onto her belly, feeling her short soft pubic hair, then down over her labia, at first covering them with her hand, then digging her fingers into the deep furrow and spreading them apart, so he would be able to see the scarlet maw of her sex.

'Is this what you want to paint?' she said.

He did not move or speak but she knew his eyes were fixed on her.

She heard an odd sound, a sucking sound. She straightened up and turned around. She strained to see him in the darkness. Now he was not alone. Betty was kneeling between his knees, the dark velvet robe pulled back, his cock buried in her mouth.

Nadine knew it was impossible. She had locked the door herself. How could Betty have got in? Was there another way in she didn't know about?

She could see Sewell's eyes were still on her, roaming the contours of her breasts, the hour-glass figure created by the basque, her long legs and her thighs bisected by the welts of the stockings. He made no attempt to stop Betty as her head bobbed rhythmically in his lap.

'I thought you wanted me.'

'I do.'

'She'll make you come.'

'That's what I want.'

'I thought you wanted me.'

'I do.'

'I'll do anything.'

'But you won't.'

'I will.'

'No.'

'I will.'

'Come here then.'

'Not with her.'

'You see. You see.'

Suddenly he was standing behind her, his rough manly hands cupping her breasts in the lacy bra of the basque, his erection, wet with Betty's saliva, probing between her buttocks, testing the tightness of the little bud of her anus, pushing harder and harder against it. He pinched her nipples so firmly the pleasure was almost painful.

'No!' she cried.

'You see,' he whispered in her ear his hot breath making her body quiver. 'You see.'

'Please . . .' she had never said the word with more emotion.

'Over here, Sewell.' Betty was kneeling on all fours on the bed, her heavy pendulous breasts grazing the sheet. Nadine could see her sex covered with its pelt of black hair. Where had the bed come from? There was a tall long-haired blonde kneeling besides her stroking the camber of Betty's buttocks. She was naked too but for white French knickers and red high heels.

'Over here, Sewell,' the blonde echoed. Sewell moved away.

'Please,' Nadine begged.

'You see,' he said. He knelt up on the bed behind Betty. Nadine saw the blonde reach for his cock, guiding it into position against the puckered crater of Betty's anus.

'Mmm . . .' Betty murmured, wriggling her hips.

'You see.'

'No, Sewell! No!'

He pushed forward and Betty threw her head back, laughing loudly.

The laughter woke her.

Nadine was covered in sweat, not cold sweat but the sweat of heated excitement. She was trembling from head to toe, just as Sewell had made her tremble, and her nipples were as hard as pebbles and throbbing as though they had been pinched. Her sex was throbbing too, a pulse that dominated her whole body, demanding attention.

Tentatively she moved her hand down between her legs. She touched her labia and felt a surge of pleasure. She pressed her finger between them and immediately felt her wetness. Her clitoris was swollen and demanding. She pushed against it with the tip of her finger and gasped aloud, so strong was the wave of pleasure that flooded through her.

She closed her eyes and saw Sewell. He was looking at her with that knowing smile. Damn him, she swore, trying to think of something else, someone else, trying to conjure up Charles and what she had done with him. But Sewell's hypnotic eyes haunted her.

As her finger unconsciously began to tap out a tempo on her clitoris, she groped in the drawer of her bedside chest until her fingers lighted on the cold plastic of the dildo. Before she had even thought about what she was doing, the head of the dildo was nosing into the gate of her sex.

'No,' she said aloud, pulling her hand away from her clitoris, wanting the word to banish the desire.

It did not. Like a naughty dog sneaking back into the room from which it had been expelled, her hand snaked back down over her belly.

'No,' she repeated but this time in a different tone, a tone that meant 'yes'. She scissored her legs apart, pressed her finger onto her clitoris again and pushed the dildo right up into her body with no subtlety or finesse. The penetration made her gasp.

She did not pull it out again. She just held it firmly up inside her as her finger worked on her clitoris. The pleasure it created, all the greater now for being denied, forced her eyes closed. There in the darkness Sewell was waiting for her with his cohorts, with Betty and the long-haired blonde in French knickers.

'No.'

She didn't want to come like this, fired by the image of Sewell, haunted by him, unable to remove him from her libido, but clearly, as her body contracted around the unyielding phallus and her finger increased the tempo on her clitoris, pushing it from side to side, she had no choice.

Chapter Five

'Come in, come in,' Barbara said holding the front door open.

Nadine had rung the doorbell at five minutes past the appointed hour.

Barbara lived in a Victorian mansion block off Kensington High Street. The block had been completely restored, redecorated and rewired and provided with every conceivable modern convenience, the sort of things usually reserved for modern flats with commensurately modern-sized rooms the size of large shoe-boxes. Barbara's flat on the other hand was vast, with imposing rooms, high ceilings and large sash windows that overlooked a well-tended private garden square. She had a natural flare for interior design and had spent a great deal of money on the flat, taking endless trouble to match colour and texture and tone in each of the rooms, spending hours searching antique shops and architectural salvage companies to find exactly the right table or chair or *objet d'art* for every nook and cranny.

Nadine kissed Barbara on both cheeks and walked into the cavernous hall, so large Barbara had a medieval reredos leaning against one wall, its delicate wooden carving lit by two spotlights which she claimed to have found in a rubbish skip. To the side of it was a coffer of a similar age, its lid shaped like a tent, each side carved in relief with some hunting scene.

'These are for you,' Nadine said. She handed Barbara a bunch of white Arum lilies.

'They're beautiful. Come on. I'll introduce you first then I'll put these in water.'

They trooped into the sitting room, a large square room which held three long Chesterfields without appearing cramped. Each Chesterfield was upholstered in a different colour and pattern of material though all three seemed to blend together naturally.

Three men and a woman sat chatting, parked comfortably on the sofas which were grouped around a gothic fireplace retrieved from a salvage yard. In the winter Barbara had wood delivered and carried up the three floors so she could have a massive log fire. At the moment, the fireplace was full of a tasteful display of dried flowers.

'Ted you already know,' Barbara said. Ted was Barbara's regular dinner companion. He worked at a rival agency, had a handshake like a wet fish and was as limp-wristed as a clichéd example of someone of his sexual orientation could possibly be. He seemed to enjoy being as camp as possible.

'Hello, darling,' he said miming kissing Nadine on both cheeks without coming anywhere near her.

'This is Mandy and Fred. You met them at that last bash.'

'I remember. How are you?'

Fred was the features editor of a tabloid

newspaper. He was short and almost bald and wore clothes that made him look like an American who had just come off the golf course, a plaid jacket and bright green cotton trousers. His wife was a dumpy little woman with bleached blond hair and a ready smile.

Nadine's eyes turned to the third man in the party, the man obviously intended to be her partner at dinner. He was slender and impeccably groomed, smelling of some cologne she did not recognise, with a neat but rather weak face. He had fair hair, parted on one side, and he was greying slightly over his ears. His eyes were a grey blue.

'This is Paul Hammond,' Barbara said nudging her friend with an elbow and little subtlety.

The man got to his feet and extended a small, carefully manicured hand.

'I'm obviously your date for tonight,' he said smiling as he shook Nadine's hand. His handshake was firm but not strong. He was about the same height as Nadine in her high heels, which was not tall for a man.

'I'll put these in water, darling,' Barbara said, avoiding the look in Nadine's eyes that was full of reproach. Barbara was always doing this, setting her up with men who turned out to be totally unsuitable. 'Pour her a drink, Paul, there's a good fellow.'

'That's a beautiful dress,' Paul said. There was an open bottle of champagne on the coffee table in front of the sofa and a spare glass. Paul poured the wine and handed the glass to Nadine who thanked him with a nod of her head.

'Gorgeous,' Ted agreed.

'Armani?' Mandy guessed.

'Yes.' Nadine confirmed. Her dress was a creamy silk, very loose-fitting with puffy chiffon sleeves. She wore white tights and cream-coloured lizard-skin shoes.

'You're in advertising?' Paul asked.

Nadine sat down in a small armchair upholstered in a grey-and-white-check print.

'Yes. Very venal. And you?'

'I'm in ILCs.' He pronounced it like the woman's name: Elsie.

'What's an Elsie?' Fred asked.

'International Letters of Credit.'

'And what on earth are they?' Ted said.

'Well . . .' Nadine looked at Paul closely. He was wearing a suit that fitted him perfectly, lying smoothly on his shoulders without a single crease, the trousers exactly the right length, the dark blue material obviously of the finest quality. His white shirt was silk with a double-stitched collar and cuffs, and his silk tie was the perfect shade of blue to complement the colour of his suit. He wore discreet silver cuff links and his watch, she noticed, was gold and as thin as a razor blade. '. . . say you're running a company making tractors and you want to export a couple of thousand to Vietnam. Well, I go to a bank and get them to agree the credit to build the tractors against the eventual payment from the Vietnamese. That way the bank takes the risk and not the manufacturing company.'

'And you get a percentage?' Nadine suggested.

'Exactly. The more difficult the deal is to arrange, which means the bigger the risk factor, the more I get.'

'It must be very interesting,' Mandy said, though she didn't sound very convincing.

'I have to do a lot of travelling.'

'Really?'

'Yes, all over the world. Africa and Asia mostly but the States too.'

'Dinner is served,' Barbara said, coming back into the room with an art-deco vase filled with the lilies which she put on a white baby-grand piano positioned near one of the tall windows.

Barbara's dining room was another example of her flair for interior design. The walls were covered in material, drawn up to a point in the centre of the ceiling to give the effect of being in a Bedouin's tent. The table setting reflected the trouble she took over appearances, the crockery and cutlery had all been chosen with enormous care, the tablecloth was a shade of dark red and the napkins, wrapped in rings made from twisted ash twigs, were of the same material. Big fat candles sitting in glass bowls, also surrounded by circles of ash twigs, flickered in the middle of the rectangular table.

They sat and talked, easily and humourlessly, eating Barbara's excellent food. They talked about advertising, Fred's experiences as a cub reporter on a tabloid paper and Paul's travels around the world. They talked about music and opera, which Nadine loved, and so did Paul.

Nadine's impression of Paul, her *first* impression,

had not been good. He struck her as weak and ineffectual, and she was not attracted to him. But then, as she knew, the measuring stick by which she judged such things had been changed drastically by Sewell. Sewell had, almost literally, knocked her off her feet. She knew she mustn't expect other men to have the same effect. Judging men by Sewell's standards was not a trap she wanted to fall into. And, as the evening progressed, she became increasingly taken with Paul. He was modest, charming and diffident and his physical appearance seemed to match his personality. He was not attractive but he was personable and, in the way of such things, the more Nadine enjoyed his company, the more she liked the look of his delicate, neat face.

The evening ended comparatively early and Barbara's offer of liqueurs was refused. Fred and Mandy left with Ted, who lived in the same direction and had begged a lift. As Barbara saw them off at the door, Nadine and Paul were left alone together for the first time.

'This is where I ask you if you'd like to have dinner with me some time,' he said, smiling.

'Yes, it is,' she agreed.

'So would you like to have dinner with me some time?'

'I don't know what Barbara's told you about me . . .'

'She told me you were divorced, that's all.'

'And you? Are you married?'

'Divorced.'

'Children?'

'No.'

'Was it a nasty divorce?'

'Can I tell you over dinner? We can compare divorces.'

'I'll think about it.'

'You're a very beautiful woman, Nadine. I'm sure most men tell you that but it doesn't make it any less true.'

'Thank you.'

There was a silence for a moment. The expression on Paul's face suggested he was hoping she'd change her mind, a little like a dog hoping he was about to be thrown a bone.

'Look, Paul,' she said finally, 'you're a nice man. I've just . . .' She tried to think of something to say that would be an adequate excuse. 'I'm just not in the market for another . . . for a man at the moment. I've had a rather bruising affair.'

'But it's over now?'

'Yes,' she said very definitely. 'But I need time to sort myself out. Maybe in a couple of weeks.'

'I understand. Can I call you?'

'That would be nice.'

He took out a slim leather notepad which had gold corners and a gold propelling pencil in a little leather loop at the side and took down her work and home numbers just as Barbara returned.

'Oh, so what's going on there then?' She asked smiling broadly.

'Absolutely nothing,' Nadine said hoping her friend would not pursue the subject.

'I must go,' Paul said. He stood up. 'It's been

wonderful to meet you,' he said to Nadine as she got up too. 'And, Barbara, such lovely food.'

'Any time.'

They both saw him off at the door.

'Well, what did you think?' Barbara said the moment the door had closed after him.

'I wish you'd told me you were fixing me up with a partner.'

'Come on, you know I won't have uneven numbers at dinner. It's just not done.'

'I'm not in the mood.'

'But he is nice, isn't he?'

'Nice is exactly right.'

'You don't think nice is good enough?'

'Barbara, to tell you the truth I don't know what I think any more.'

'He's stinking rich.'

'Does that make a difference?'

'It would to me. Unfortunately I'm two feet too tall for him. We'd look silly together. But you . . . you gave him your number?'

'That doesn't mean I'm going to go out with him.'

'Of course it doesn't.'

'We'll see.'

'Oh, we certainly will.'

'Hi.'

'Hello?'

Nadine had picked up the phone in the hall just as she was about to walk out the front door.

'Not too early, is it?'

'I was just going to work.' She was trying to

recognise the voice but couldn't. 'Sorry, who is this?'

'Paul. Paul Hammond. The dinner party, remember?'

'Oh yes. How are you?' She said it automatically. In fact, she was annoyed. It was only two days since Barbara's dinner and she'd told him to wait weeks.

'Fine, I'm fine. Look I know I was supposed to wait before I called you but I remember you said over dinner you loved opera. Well, I've got two tickets for *La Traviata* with Solti conducting. They're like gold. I just thought . . .'

Nadine hesitated. *Traviata* was her favourite opera. She hadn't seen it announced in either the programmes for the season at the Coliseum or Covent Garden but perhaps this was a special gala.

'When is it?'

'That's the thing, I'm afraid it's tomorrow.'

'Tomorrow?' Tomorrow was Saturday and she had nothing planned.

'I know what you said. I thought we could just do the opera. Nothing else. We can even skip dinner, I'll bring you straight home. I don't want to break the rules.'

Nadine laughed. 'No, if I'm going I'd like dinner too. I love *Traviata*.'

'I'll have to pick you up early.'

'How early?'

'Five thirty.'

'Why's that?'

'It's too complicated to explain over the phone. Is five thirty OK?'

'I could meet you there.'

'No, it's better that I come and pick you up.'
'If you're sure . . .'
'Dress to the nines. It's a big do.'
'Fine.' She gave him her address. 'See you then.'
'I'm looking forward to it,' he said.
'But Paul . . .'
'Yes.'
'Don't expect me to sleep with you.'
'I told you I wasn't even expecting you to have dinner.'

The moment she put the phone down she regretted accepting the offer. It would be marvellous to see the opera but she was not in the mood to get involved with another man. The spectre of Sewell still haunted her. She thought about him all the time, the images of his paintings and the memory of what had happened merging together. Art and reality were so confused she could hardly distinguish between the two. But both had the same effect, leaving her body throbbing and needy.

Though she was adamant in her own mind that she did not want to expose herself to Sewell again, physically or mentally, to allow those dark eyes to draw her into the complex web of his unorthodox life, neither did she want the feelings and emotions he provoked to dissipate. Not yet anyway. It was perverse but another man, another affair, would inevitably distance her from Sewell.

It *was* perverse. She didn't have to be distanced from Sewell at all. She could have him now. Immediately. All she had to do was pick up the phone. Not even that. She could just drive around to his house. He wouldn't reject her. He'd lead her up to the bedroom where Betty would be waiting. Betty would smile as she helped her take off her clothes. She'd touch her body. She'd kiss her. She'd prepare her for Sewell.

And that's exactly what Nadine didn't want. She wanted Sewell, wanted him more than any man she'd ever wanted in her entire life, but not like that. She wanted him on her own terms, not on his. That's what it amounted to.

Of course it was more complicated than that. Since the night with Betty, Nadine had slept badly. She had lain awake trying to work out precisely what her reactions were to what had happened and, hard as she'd tried, she had barely got to first base. Had Betty excited her, thrilled her, made her come, because somehow Betty had been an extension of Sewell? Or maybe her experience with the brunette meant something else entirely. Did she really want to have sex with a woman? It was a question she could not resolve.

Sewell had had another effect on her too. Whereas, before Sewell, sex had been a small and unsatisfactory part of her life, placed firmly on the back burner, occasionally bubbling to the surface, and mostly – if she were honest – tolerated as a necessary function of a relationship with men, now it seemed to have a life of its own. It was a monster on the loose, gaining strength and energy from a diet of daily stimulation.

Suddenly Nadine seemed aware of sex, of couples kissing on street corners, of scenes on television, of nude and semi-nude pictures in magazines, of lingerie in shop windows. Sex was everywhere. Four or five times a day she would see an image that would make her melt inside, that would reduce the compass of her life to the narrow crease between her legs, that would make her acutely aware of her body's sudden arousal and, ultimately, would conjure up images of Sewell or one of his paintings.

She had found she was masturbating almost every day. She had no choice. She needed it. And every night she used the dildo too, sometimes just as a phallus, sometimes with the vibrator turned on but always with it crammed into her body as far as it would go. What's more the results were shattering. She came like she had never come before, perhaps not as dramatically as she had with Sewell, but with a force and power that made her senses reel.

It was always Sewell whom she imagined inside her, always Sewell the plastic phallus deputised for. But, despite her efforts not to bring her into the equation, it was often Betty, her smile or her soft brown eyes or her artful tongue, that was the final vision she saw before orgasm engulfed her.

That was Sewell's real legacy.

She locked her front door and got into her car, trying to expel the thoughts that had forced their way to the fore once again. At least a night at the opera would take her away from her humdrum routine.

She had no idea quite how far.

The doorbell rang at exactly half past five.

Nadine had taken Paul at his word. She was wearing a strapless full-length black dress that clung to her figure from her bust to her knees, where it flared out slightly and had a kick pleat which enabled her to walk more easily. The material was woven with a silver thread which made the dress glisten as it caught the light. The neckline of the dress offered an alluring view of Nadine's firm cleavage. She carried, and would wear later, elbow length gloves in the same material. Around her neck she wore a modern silver choker with long silver earrings to match, her hair pinned up to reveal her long graceful neck. The lines and tightness of the dress would not allow her to wear any lingerie so she was simply wearing very sheer tights.

'Hi,' she said opening the door.

'You look fabulous.'

'You said go to town.'

'Fabulous.'

'Do you want a drink before we leave?'

'We don't have time. Sorry but it's a carefully planned military operation. Seconds count.'

'Fine.'

Nadine locked her front door, dropped the keys into a small evening bag and, very deliberately, took Paul's arm. It was a gesture to herself more than to him. She wanted to anchor herself to him for the evening, to have a night off from images of Sewell.

To her astonishment, double-parked in the small suburban road was a black, immaculately polished Rolls Royce. A uniformed chauffeur stood by the passenger door, which he opened as they approached.

'This is Vernon,' Paul said.

'Good evening, Miss,' Vernon said politely, tipping his grey chauffeur's cap. He was a small compact man with very short legs and a rather serious face.

They climbed into the back seat and Nadine inhaled the expensive aroma of leather and walnut veneer. There was a glass partition behind the front seats.

Vernon closed the rear door with a heavy clunk and the car moved off noiselessly, the soft suspension making it feel as though they were floating on air.

'What a lovely car,' Nadine said as they drove. After a few minutes she realised they were driving out of town. 'Where are we going?'

'You'll see,' Paul said with a smile. 'That's a beautiful dress.'

'Thank you.'

Paul picked up a phone built into the leather armrest, punched in a number and waited. 'We'll be there in twenty minutes,' he said, then put the phone down again.

The car soon reached the motorway. Nadine guessed they were going to Glyndebourne for some special gala event but when they began to travel west she realised she must be wrong.

It was a hot evening and in the tight dress Nadine was grateful for the car's air conditioning. This was definitely the way to travel.

'This is very intriguing,' she said.

'Just a little surprise.'

She looked out of the window, trying to find a clue to their destination. At first she thought they were going to Heathrow but then the Rolls turned north. It was another ten minutes before they pulled into the entrance of a small private airfield. The security guard swung the gates open and the car accelerated onto the tarmac where a white Learjet stood on the taxiway, its engines running.

The chauffeur swung the big car round so that Nadine's door was next to the plane's landing steps, then got out and opened the door for her. A uniformed steward in a white linen jacket appeared at the door of the plane.

'Where are we going?' Nadine repeated. She could not help but be impressed.

'It'll take about twenty-five minutes. I'll tell you if you don't like surprises.'

'No, no . . . I think I'd like to be surprised. You're doing well so far.'

Nadine was feeling a little dazed. The Rolls and the chauffeur had been unexpected enough but a private plane was even more difficult to cope with. When Barbara had said Paul was rich, Nadine hadn't imagined it was on this scale.

'Good old EC. Before 1994 I'd have had to ask you to bring your passport, which would have given the game away. Not now though . . .'

Trying to appear unabashed Nadine got out of the car and mounted the steps of the plane with Paul at her heels.

'Good evening, Madam, Sir . . .' the steward said. 'May I get you a drink before take-off?'

'Champagne I think,' Paul said and Nadine nodded in agreement. Her first flight in a private plane certainly had to be accompanied by champagne.

The interior of the plane was as luxurious as the Rolls had been. There was a leather sofa and three large, comfortable armchairs. On the wall was a television with a video player beneath it. There was a telephone and a CD player with speakers set into the bulkhead. The floor was covered in thick wool carpets.

Nadine sat in one of the armchairs and did up her seat belt. The chair, despite its size, swivelled so she could turn to the window or face the interior of the cabin with ease. Paul sat opposite her.

'Very impressive,' she said.

He grinned like a schoolboy showing off his favourite toy. Nadine found the grin endearing. If he had appeared blasé about all this she didn't think she would have liked him as much. But his obvious delight in what his wealth could provide made her feel an unexpected streak of affection for him.

The steward brought two glasses of champagne.

'The call button's on the arm of the seats, Sir, if there's anything else you require. I suggest you hold the glasses during take-off.' He closed the outer door and disappeared into the forward cabin as the noise of the engines increased and the plane started to roll forward.

'Good evening. This is the captain.' The voice sounded through the cabin. 'We've just been cleared for take-off. Our journey time will be twenty minutes and we don't anticipate any delays. The inertial navigation system has a repeater display on the television screen. Should you wish to know our position, press for Channel 10. I hope you have a pleasant flight.'

'Would you like to see our position?' Paul said with glee.

'I definitely think so.' Nadine said.

He got up and turned the television on, pressing the appropriate button on the channel selector. A map of Europe appeared; the land mass in green, the ocean in blue with a little red airplane symbol stationary over London. Figures in the bottom of the screen noted their air speed, height and the outside temperature. They read 0, 10 ft, and 74F.

Paul settled back in his chair and fastened his seat belt. The plane turned onto the runway and, in a surge of speed and roar from the tail-mounted engines, they were airborne. As they climbed rapidly the figures on the television screen changed accordingly.

'Is this your plane?'

Paul laughed. 'No, no. I'm not that rich. I hire it from time to time. Is it your first trip in a private plane?'

'Yes. It's wonderful.'

Nadine examined Paul closely as she sipped her champagne. Though she liked him she couldn't honestly say she was attracted to him. It was fortunate she had prohibited any sexual activity as a condition of acceptance because the idea of going to bed with him, while not exactly repellent, was definitely not exciting.

The aircraft on the screen moved to the east of

London and was soon heading out over the Channel.
It did not take a genius to work out the number of
destinations available to the east on a twenty-minute
flight and only one had an opera house where George
Solti was likely to perform.

'We're going to Paris,' Nadine declared.

'Got it in one.'

'How lovely.'

'I thought you'd like it. Have you been before?'

'In my student days. The opera house has got that
marvellous Chagall on the ceiling.'

'Yes, and I've booked a table at the Grand Véfour.'

The steward arrived as soon as the plane had
levelled out and placed a plate of canapés on the low
table in front of them. There was caviar, smoked
salmon and quails' eggs. He topped up their glasses
with champagne. This was definitely the way to
travel.

A large American limousine waited for them at
L'Aeroporte Charles de Gaulle and they drove
rapidly into the heart of Paris arriving at L'Opera
with twenty minutes to spare. They were shown to
a box on the left side of the auditorium.

Nadine was feeling a little dizzy at all the luxury
but soon settled into the world of the lady of the
camellias and forgot everything else. The swelling
strings of Verdi, the beautiful heart-rending tunes
and the superb voices made everything else in the
world seem, for the time being, insignificant.

The limousine was waiting outside and they were
whisked to the old-fashioned splendour of the Grand
Véfour, decorated in gilt and red with numerous

long mirrors behind most of the banquettes.

Paul ordered champagne, a vintage Tattinger, which arrived at the table in an elaborate *fin de siècle* silver wine-cooler.

'Cheers,' he said.

'Thank you, Paul,' Nadine said. 'This is all too much. The opera was wonderful.'

Nadine's mood had been changed, perhaps by all Paul's arrangements, but more probably by the opera itself. She felt Paul had shared its dramatic impact. He had appeared as moved by it as she was. They had both shed a tear and Nadine had always liked a man who was prepared to show his feelings. That wasn't quite true. She had always *said* she liked a man who showed his feelings, but Paul was the first she had ever spent any time with.

The more they talked, the more she found she liked him. He was knowledgeable about music, food and wine but had a self-depreciating manner that she liked. He had a way of seeming totally fascinated by everything she said.

The food was as good as the opera had been and the wine, a rich Burgundy Paul had chosen to go with the *ballotine de canard*, quite exceptional. By the end of the meal Nadine's sense of well-being was as expansive as her mood. She refused the offer of liqueurs but they did indulge in a glass of Chateau Y'quem.

'Well,' Paul said as they toyed with petits fours and coffee, 'I suppose I'd better get you back to London.'

'That was a question, I hope.'

'What, had I better take you back to London?'

'Exactly. The night is young and we've come all this way . . .'

'Couldn't have put it better myself.'

'What do you suggest?'

'A club?'

'Sounds like fun . . .' Nadine did not want the evening to end. It had been exciting and the thought of driving home through the streets of London was an anticlimax she didn't want to contemplate just yet. 'Have you got one in mind?'

'Well . . .' He hesitated. 'There's a nice bar on the *rive gauche*.'

'Or?'

'There is a club.' She thought he was starting to blush.

'What sort of club?'

'No, I shouldn't have mentioned it.'

'What sort of club?'

'It has performances.'

'Sex. That's what Paris is famous for, isn't it? Have you been there before?'

'Yes. It's very *outré*.'

Much to her surprise, Nadine found herself saying, 'Take me there.'

'No, I don't think . . .'

'Paul, I mean it. Come on. It would interest me.' She meant it too. For some reason the idea of some sort of sex show appealed to her very much. She had come out with the specific idea of having a total rest from even a passing thought about sex but now she had changed her mind.

144

'I didn't think we were going to have that sort of relationship,' Paul said quietly.

Nadine laid her hand on top of Paul's on the table. It was the first time they'd touched all evening. 'I don't know that we are . . .'

'I didn't mean I thought . . .'

'I know what you meant, Paul, and you're right. So just take me to this club and let's see what happens.' She knew that was a come-on but she didn't care. She'd made it quite clear to Paul that sex was not on the agenda tonight. If she wanted to change her mind that was her privilege and, if she didn't, he would just have to live with his disappointment. She liked Paul but she didn't care about him enough to want to be less ambiguous. Not yet anyway.

Paul paid the bill and they walked out to the car which was parked under the fan-shaped glass and metal awning. Paul gave the driver directions and five minutes later they were pulling up outside what looked like a private house in a road that appeared to have no commercial premises of any kind. There was no sign or light over the front door.

Paul rang the doorbell. The heavy door swung open immediately. Taking a card from his wallet he showed it to the doorman who stood aside to let him in.

'Do you have to be a member?' Nadine whispered as they walked through the door.

'Yes,' he said, a little guiltily she thought.

They found themselves in a small square space surrounded by heavy red velvet curtains that hung down from the ceiling. The doorman parted the curtaining and disappeared but almost before the curtains had fallen back into place they were opened again and a tall slender blonde appeared. She was wearing a leotard made from leather so soft it looked like cloth, and cut so high most of the creases of the girl's pelvis were on display under a covering of black fishnet tights. The boots she was wearing were made from the same sort of leather and stretched up to her thigh.

'*Bon soir. Suivez,*' she said opening the curtain and leading the way.

They followed her down a dimly lit staircase and into a cavernous cellar. There was a bar at one end and a small stage at the other. In between there were tables surrounded by gilt chairs with a candle set in an oval glass bowl in the middle of each.

The blonde showed them to a table.

'*Vous desirez quelque chose?*'

'Champagne,' Paul said.

On the stage a three-piece band played a series of standards and the pianist improvised on the main themes with a great deal of skill.

Nadine watched the other waitresses, all dressed in the same outlandish costumes, their buttocks almost completely exposed by the leotards' thin crotchpiece, as they plied the tables. The club was full of couples, though a few single men sat on stools at the bar.

As their champagne arrived, the lights in the club dimmed and spotlights illuminated the stage. A woman, dressed in a man's dinner suit and black tie, stepped out from the wings carrying a microphone.

'*Bon soir, bon soir, mesdames et messieurs*, ladies and gentlemen, for your pleasure, *pour votre plaisir, nous presentons*, Adeline . . .'

The band played softly as a petite redhead stepped onto the stage. She was wearing a tight-fitting black lace blouse and a long black skirt and carrying a gilt chair. She put the chair in the middle of the stage and immediately put one of her feet, shod in spiky black high heels, up on its seat, raising her skirt until the audience could see that she was wearing stockings, their welts held in place by black satin suspenders.

She did what Nadine imagined, having never seen one before, was a fairly standard striptease, removing her blouse and skirt in time to the music. The more she took off, the more uneasy Paul became.

As the compère came back on stage he leant over to Nadine and whispered, 'I'm not sure this is such a good idea.'

'Why not? It's fun.'

He shrugged.

The compère was holding a short leather riding-crop. The stripper removed her bra to reveal very small breasts with disproportionately large nipples and was left in a thin black satin suspender-belt and a pair of black satin panties. She reversed the chair so the back was nearest to the audience then bent over it, pushing her fleshy buttocks out, so her hands grasped the seat and the top of the chair pressed into her waist.

The compère stood beside her. She raised the riding crop and whacked it down on the girl's satin-covered rump.

The redhead yelled exaggeratedly.

'*Mesdames et messieurs*, ladies and gentlemen, and now,*et maintenant, un volontaire* – a volunteer?'

There were cheers from the crowd and two or three hands went up. The compère pointed at one of the tables and a tall fat man staggered unsteadily up the three wooden steps to one side of the stage. He took the whip and smacked it down on the redhead who yelled with equal fervour, though it was obvious that the man had used no real power.

As the man tottered back to his seat the compère pointed again and a gaunt-looking man with hollow cheeks and thinning hair took the whip from her. He took the business altogether more seriously, raised his arm high and slashed the whip down with a thwack that reverberated through the room. The girl yelled with more feeling. The audience applauded loudly.

The compère pointed again. To Nadine's surprise this time it was a woman who wound her way between the tables. She was slender and elegant, her auburn hair pinned in a neat chignon to the back of her head, her body encased in a tight-fitting blue suit, the skirt of which was split to reveal a great deal of thigh. She mounted the steps and came over to the girl taking the whip from the compère's hand.

But she did not raise it immediately as the men had done. First she walked all the way around the girl and stroked her back. Then she took the waistband of the satin panties and, to applause from the audience, pulled them down over the girl's buttocks until they were bunched around her thighs. The girl's bottom was reddened by the previous blows but there were no distinct weals.

The woman's hand caressed the tender flesh and the girl wriggled her hips from side to side. Nadine could see, where the panties still clung to her crotch, a profuse growth of red pubic hair.

The woman raised the whip. The crowd encouraged her with cries of *'Oui'* and *'Faites'* and the whip whistled down across the redhead's plump buttocks, this time leaving a long thin red weal and making the girl gasp in pain. Two more strokes followed. The woman caressed the weals she had made, making the redhead gasp again. Then she pulled her up from the chair and cupped one of her breasts in her hand, pinching its nipple between her fingers. The girl looked puzzled but the woman's other hand grasped her cheeks and pulled her face into a kiss, opening her mouth and kissing her hard, her tongue clearly forcing its way between her lips.

Nadine's reaction to this was a shock of sensation so strong it was as though she had been slapped. She was glad the lighting in the club was dim because she was sure her face was a bright red. She felt her sex pulse so strongly that she, too, almost gasped.

The audience applauded and shouted *'Encore, encore.'* They got what they wanted.

The woman handed the redhead the whip and calmly unzipped her skirt, stepping out of it before it fell to the floor and handing it to the compère. She was wearing sheer grey-coloured tights with little white panties on top. She bent over the chair just as the girl had done, the jacket of the suit short enough to expose the whole of her pert but slender bottom, divided neatly by the back of the panties which was really no more than a thin string buried in the cleft of her buttocks.

The redhead immediately raised the whip and swung it down on the woman's nylon-covered rump. The stroke was hard and the woman made a peculiar hissing sound. The redhead was not satisfied. She got hold of the waistband of the tights and pulled them down, necessarily pulling the panties down too. With the tights around the woman's thighs, the red weal the first stroke had created was quite clear. Two more followed on the bare flesh, each followed by the woman's strange sibilant cry.

Handing the whip to the compère the redhead ran her hands over the woman's buttocks and Nadine heard her gasp. Then she pulled the tights up, smoothing them back into place and helped the woman to straighten up. There was, Nadine thought, a look of complicity between them. Either this had been pre-arranged or the brief exchange had stirred something in both women that would need to be satisfied later.

To the applause of the audience the woman climbed back into her skirt and left the stage, rejoining her companion, a middle-aged man, who greeted her return enthusiastically.

The house lights went up again and the stage lights dimmed as the band began to play 'Misty'.

'Perhaps we should go,' Paul said.

'Why?'

'It's not what I was expecting.'

'I thought you'd been here before.'

'I had. But it wasn't like this . . .'

'Like what?'

'S and M.'

'What's S and M?'

'Sado-masochism.'

'I'm not embarrassed, Paul. Let's stay. It's an education.'

Paul took a large gulp of his champagne. Nadine wasn't at all sure what was going on in his mind. She felt it was unlikely that he didn't know the sort of acts that were featured at the club. Why had he brought her here, in that case? He could have taken her to more conventional shows like the *Crazy Horse* or the *Folies* but he had obviously wanted to bring her here and now had changed his mind.

Nadine's own reaction to what had happened, after the initial shock which had surged through her body, was curiosity tinged with a streak of excitement. How deep the streak ran she could not tell; her excitement was too entangled with the way the women had kissed, their bodies momentarily pressed together as hers and Betty's had been. She didn't know whether she was responding to the memory of the way a woman had felt against her or to the sado-masochistic element. She did know that only two weeks ago she would have walked out of here without a moment's thought, not through disgust but through boredom. Now, born again as it were, she was fascinated.

The house lights faded again and the compère reappeared.

'*Et maintenant*, and now, Pierre and Madeline . . .'

The stage was suddenly plunged into darkness. When the lights faded up again a curtain had been brought in to hide the band so the stage was quite empty. Very slowly, from above the stage, a pair of naked feet appeared, followed by the legs and torso of a man, a very muscular athletic-looking man, his genitals covered with a small triangle of stiff black leather. As his body descended and his feet touched the floor of the stage, Nadine saw that his wrists were bound together with a white rope which had been attached to a metal hook. The hook hung from a chain that disappeared up above the stage.

As she looked at the man's near-naked body, its muscles straining and flexed by bondage, Nadine felt her sex pulse for the second time that evening. Once again it was impossible for her not to think of Sewell. She shifted uneasily on the gilt chair, beginning to think that Paul had been right after all and that they should have left.

The man's head was covered with a leather hood which was laced at the back so the leather was pulled tight against his face, outlining his features. There were holes cut for his eyes and his mouth. His eyes seemed to be looking directly at Nadine.

Using the rope from which he was suspended like a piece of gymnastic equipment, the man began to struggle, lifting his legs up against his chest, jack-knifing his feet until they were above his head, his muscles straining. His body turned and Nadine saw his bottom, the thong that held the leather of his genitals cutting so deeply into the cleft of his buttocks that it was only visible where it emerged to join the equally thin waistband.

A woman strode onto the stage. She was dressed in the same tight-fitting leather boots as the waitresses but with panties made from leather and as small as the ones the man was wearing. Her firm round breasts were naked but something was attached to each of her nipples, some sort of clip from which hung a long tear-shaped silver pendant. Her hair was long and black, brushed out straight and parted in the middle, and over her eyes she wore a mask that looked as though it too were made from silver. In her left hand she carried a bullwhip, its lash coiled in rings like a snake.

The audience applauded her appearance loudly and there were shouts of '*Le Fouet*'. Nadine had the impression they all knew what was going to happen next.

'What does it mean,' she whispered to Paul.

'The Whip,' he replied without taking his eyes off the stage.

The man had stopped struggling and the brunette came to stand next to him, turning him on the hook to face the audience again.

'*Bon soir, mon chéri amour.*'

He said nothing.

She stroked her right hand over his leather-covered cheek and down his neck to his chest.

'*Es-tu confortable?*' she mocked. Her long red

varnished nails pinched at his left nipple. *'Es-tu confortable?'* she insisted.

She unclipped one of the pendants from her nipple. Nadine saw her shudder visibly as the metal jaws were freed. She positioned the clip over the man's nipple and let the jaws sink into the puckered flesh. The man moaned. He moaned again as the second clip bit into him.

'Il vaut mieux,' she said.

Her hand turned him again and she began to cup and caress his tight hard buttocks.

'Fouettez, fouettez...' came the shouts from the audience.

'Taisez-vous,' she replied.

Nadine found herself clutching Paul's arm. Her body was throbbing. It wasn't entirely because she imagined the man was Sewell, that she had not been able to escape his spectre even for one day. There was another element. She wanted to see this man whipped.

'Do you want to go?' Paul said, the pressure of her fingers alarming him.

'No,' she said, the quickness of her reply betraying her. 'No,' she said more slowly, 'I'm fine. Don't worry.'

The woman on stage stepped back, let the coils of the whip fall from her hand and then cracked the whip across the man's near naked bottom with a noise that sounded almost like a gun shot. Four times in quick succession she cracked the whip, each lash greeted with cat-calls of approval from the audience. Four long, thin scarlet weals appeared on the man's buttocks.

The woman dropped the whip to shouts from the audience who wanted more. She went back to the man and slowly turned him to face the audience again. As his genitals came into view Nadine could see that his penis was now fully erect and had worked its way out of the leather covering, so half of it was exposed. The sight was greeted by cries of approval from the crowd.

The woman pulled the leather pouch down over the man's hips. It dropped to the floor, freeing his erection. Her hand caressed the weals on his buttocks and his cock jerked spectacularly. She flicked the two silver pendants with the same result.

She dropped to her knees in front of him. Just like the leather pouch on the man, the thong of her tiny leather panties was almost hidden in the cleft of her buttocks. She ran her hand down over the rich curves and Nadine could see her fingers penetrate her own sex at exactly the same moment she sucked his cock into her mouth. At exactly that moment the lights were blacked out too.

After a few seconds the house lights came up and the man and woman had disappeared. The curtain around the band had been hoisted away and the three men were taking their places again. They began playing 'Send in the Clowns'. There was a small dance floor in front of the stage and couples began to dance, or at least mooch around the floor with their arms wrapped around each other. All the couples, without exception, were made up of very attractive women and older, not very prepossessing men.

Nadine looked at Paul in flickering candlelight, trying to read his expression. It was not difficult to see that the display had excited him but he was trying to hide it, in case Nadine did not share the same feeling. But she did. She had never seen anything like it in her life. She had thought the memory of Sewell, disturbing her carefully planned evening of studiously ignoring him, would have upset her. But the spectre of Sewell had faded in the face of what she had actually seen. If she were honest with herself she had found the spectacle exciting. She had been sorry when it was over. Like so much that had happened in the past two weeks she was astonished at her own reactions.

'What is this place?' she asked Paul, taking a large slug of her champagne.

'Just a club.'

'Specialising in, what did you call it?'

'S and M. Yes. Sometimes. Other nights they have other things.'

'Other things?'

'They cater for other tastes.'

'Is this your taste?' As soon as she'd said it she wished she hadn't. She didn't really want to know the answer.

'No,' he said too quickly for it to be true. 'I shouldn't have brought you here.'

'You should. I've never seen anything like this. I can't say I didn't find it exciting. I'm beginning to think I've led a very sheltered life.'

Nadine had thought that her excitement might calm down but instead she felt that odd fluttering sensation in the pit of her stomach.

'Can we go?' she asked.

'There's more . . .' he said.

'I'd like to go, Paul.' She grasped his hand. It was cold from the champagne glass. 'I don't want to go back to London,' she said, turning his hand round and lacing her fingers into his. 'Will you take me to a hotel?' From the way she said it there was no doubt that she meant 'Will you take me to bed?'

'I thought you said . . .'

'I know what I said. Women are entitled to change their minds, aren't they?' Taking the initiative with men was becoming a habit with her.

'Yes, but I thought you didn't . . .'

'Sh . . .' She put a finger to his lips then lent forward and kissed his cheek. It was the last thing she'd imagined doing tonight, the last she imagined doing with Paul, but she needed sex. She needed it badly in a way she had that night with Charles. It was a physical need. She didn't need Paul, not as a person. He just happened to be on hand.

'We don't need to go to a hotel. I've got an apartment on Avenue Foch.'

'What are we waiting for then?' Being this direct seemed to increase Nadine's excitement.

Paul looked astonished and unhappy. However he had expected the evening to end, it was definitely not like this. Perhaps he was the sort of man who had to feel he'd made a conquest, who didn't like women being so blatant – particularly when they had previously made it so clear that they would not entertain the idea of sex. But Nadine didn't care.

She was not interested in his feelings, only her own. There was a freedom about that which was yet another new experience on her growing list.

He paid the bill with an American Express Gold Card and slipped a large denomination note into the waitress's hand.

Outside the limousine waited, the driver springing to the back door as soon as he saw them emerge from the front door of the club.

They settled into the back of the car. Nadine took Paul's hand but neither said a word. The silence was thick with implications.

It was no more than a five-minute drive to the Avenue Foch along the wide and deserted boulevards of Paris. The car swept into a semi-circular drive in front of a large detached house.

As they got out of the car Paul took a small key-ring from his pocket. 'I hadn't planned this,' he said.

'I know that,' Nadine replied.

He opened the glass-and-wrought-iron front door. The hall beyond had high ceilings and a stone floor. A sweeping stone staircase, the central section of its steps carpeted in a burgundy red, led up to the first floor. Judging by the neatly stacked mail boxes to the left of the hall the huge building had been divided into four *appartements*.

Paul led the way up to the first floor. He opened one of a pair of massive double doors.

The door opened onto a wide hall floored in marble. To the left, the doors to the sitting room were open. The room was decorated in a typically French style, with Louis XV furniture and gilt mirrors and a wooden parquet floor.

Paul was about to lead her into here when she caught his hand.

'No,' she said. 'Where's the bedroom?'

'Second on the right,' he replied.

Nadine had never behaved like this. She felt as though she was intoxicated but not with alcohol. She was intoxicated with an exhilaration that had coursed through her body since the scenes at the club. It was even stronger now, feeding on itself.

They walked down the hall and opened the door to the bedroom. Nadine turned the light switch on. It lit two big chunky lamps on either side of the bed. It was on a dimmer which she operated until the room was bathed in a pleasant glow.

The master bedroom was as lavish as she might have expected, a big double bed with a heavy canopy jutting out from the wall. The carpet was deep blue and thick, the walls covered in pale blue silk.

Paul followed her into the room.

'Very nice,' she said. She had never before barged through a man's home straight to the bedroom, and never had she treated a man as she was treating Paul. In the past she had always observed the conventions, and let the man do the running, climbing the rungs of the ladder of seduction, from kissing, to stroking, to touching her breasts, to easing off her clothes, never quite sure whether they would step on a snake and slide back to the beginning. But tonight she wasn't in the mood for games. What she wanted was too raw for such cautious behaviour, too raw and too urgent.

Her long dress had a zip at the side. She unhooked the catch at the top and pulled it down. She wriggled out of the garment and hung it over the back of a small sofa that stood in front of the curtained windows. Then she turned to face Paul in her sheer black tights and high heels, presenting him with the challenge of her body. Her breasts still quivered slightly from her movement, the corrugated flesh of her nipples already stiff from her exhilaration.

'You're very lovely,' Paul said, his voice sounding hoarse.

Nadine said nothing. She stripped the counterpane off the bed, pulled back the top sheet, then kicked off her shoes. She could feel her pulse hammering out a rhythm in her ears. She felt an odd sense of power, of authority, of being totally in control. Like everything else that was happening, it excited her.

'Aren't you going to take your clothes off?' she said and sat on the edge of the bed.

He pulled off his jacket and tie and began unbuttoning his shirt. Nadine watched, knowing she was making him self-conscious but not caring.

'I've got to use the bathroom,' he said walking over to a door opposite the foot of the bed and closing it firmly behind him.

Nadine rolled the tights off her legs and lay on the bed, propping her head against the pillows. Her body was alive, literally humming like an electric motor and it felt as though it was vibrating. She spread her legs and ran a finger between her labia. She was not at all surprised to find herself wet.

Without any hesitation she teased her clitoris out and stroked it with her finger. The humming in her body increased, raised by a semi-tone. With her legs apart, she felt the mouth of her sex, its sensitive tissue slick and slippery, her need all too obvious. She was tempted to plunge her fingers into her vagina but resisted. What she needed was a man.

The bathroom door opened and Paul appeared, a small white towel wrapped around his waist. His body was slim with no noticeable muscle. His skin was tanned though and lightly covered with fair, almost blond, hair. The expression on his face was quizzical.

'Are you sure this is what you want?' he said, approaching the side of the bed and looking at her naked body.

'Yes, Paul, it's exactly what I want.' It wasn't, of course. She wanted the tough, muscular body of the man she had seen on stage.

She moved her finger to the side so he would be able to see what she was doing to her clitoris.

'Would you like me to do that?' he asked quietly.

'Mmm . . .' she replied, taking her hand away. 'I'm behaving like a whore,' she said. 'Are you shocked?'

'No.'

She couldn't tell from his tone of voice or his expression whether that was true or not. But once again she discovered she didn't care.

He sat on the edge of the bed and extended his hand to her knee. He stroked upward until he was at the crease of her pelvis. He looked at her again as if to reassure himself that this was what she wanted.

She wriggled her hips so his hand nudged her belly.

He pressed his finger down between her legs and into her labia. Rather inexpertly he searched for her clitoris, his finger too low.

'Higher up,' she instructed. She had always been careful of what she said to men in bed for fear of hurting their feelings or bruising their masculinity but not tonight.

His finger nosed higher and she felt a shock of pleasure as it touched her clitoris.

'Yes, oh yes, that's it,' she said to make sure he didn't move away.

'Like this,' he asked circling the little promontory. He appeared willing to take instruction.

'No,' she said brazenly. 'Like this . . .' She put her finger on top of his and moved it from side to side. Her body trembled. She took her hand away and he continued in the way she'd demonstrated.

'Lovely, lovely . . .' she said, meaning it.

He was pressing with exactly the right pressure. She had already brought herself halfway to orgasm. Her newfound assertiveness, the personality she was testing – brash, needy, wanton – had seen to that. He was rapidly taking her the rest of the way. She wanted to come badly. She wanted to come for herself but at the same time she wanted to come for him, to show him how responsive she could be and how open.

His finger moved on the exact path she had chosen for it. She looked up into his eyes. He was looking at her sex, his face set in determined concentration. Her body tightened. She raised her hips, her body arched off the bed.

'You're coming,' he said.

'Yes, watch me, Paul . . .'

She hid nothing. She held nothing back. He was a stranger but she let him see her most private moment, the shuddering, slithering slide into her climax, her mouth open, a whispered 'oh' on her lips and in her throat, her eyes fluttering, the sinews of her neck like cords of rope as she pressed her head back onto the bed and her muscles locked around the central core of her sex. But he could not see what was in her mind, he could not see the man with his hands bound being lowered to the stage, his muscles stretched and strained, his buttocks trembling as the lash of the whip caught their full meat, he could not know that was what had made her come.

The orgasm gripped her, its tentacles wrapping themselves around her limbs, unwilling to let even the slightest sensation escape. Eventually, however, the grip slackened and her body slumped back on the bed.

She opened her eyes. Paul was looking into her face, worried by the power of what he had seen.

'Are you alright,' he asked.

'Of course.'

She rolled onto her side and caught hold of the knot that held the towel around his waist, stripping it away. She pulled him back until he was lying across the bed. His cock was semi-erect, surrounded by a thin patch of pubic hair. He was uncircumcised and his foreskin still covered his glans.

Nadine got to her knees, and without any hesitation, slipped his cock into her mouth. Her body was still high, humming like a tuning fork that had been struck hard, and still needy. What she needed now was what she had between her lips. She moved her hand to cup his balls. She felt his cock jerk, engorging slowly. Pulling her head away she used her hand to tug his foreskin back, then rubbed her finger over the ridge of his glans, its sensitivity greater for being protected. Paul moaned, his phallus swelling dramatically.

'That's what I want,' she said swinging her thigh over his hips and using her hand to position it between her labia. She held it there using the muscles of her sex to grip it. 'Do you want me?'

'Very much,' he said, looking up at her. He could see the tip of his cock disappearing between her legs. He reached up to grasp both her breasts.

She sank down on her haunches, watching his face as he was engulfed by her, feeling his hardness invade and become part of her as her sex folded around him. She shuddered, the action awaking echoes of her first orgasm. She pulled herself back up, then began riding him, bouncing gently up and down on him, on the pommel of his cock, each stroke longer, his cock going deeper, until she could feel her clitoris pounding against him and his glans was deep inside her.

'Come for me,' she said.

'Nadine . . .' Her name sounded strange on his lips, as strange as the person she had become.

It wasn't Paul that was coming but her. This is what she had needed, this is what she had wanted since they'd left the club – hard, hot cock. Her first orgasm had been the prelude to this, opening her up, allowing her to feel more, to take him deeper. The muscles of her sex were contracting around him in a rhythm they dictated themselves, using him, using the feel of him, for their own benefit. Nadine felt herself tense, felt her body change gear sharply and suddenly. She changed from being able to think and reason and imagine what she wanted, to not being able to think at all and in seconds she was rushing to meet the wave of her orgasm, running towards it, wanting to crash into it, before it crashed into her.

She pushed herself down onto his cock, splaying her legs apart, grinding herself against him using every muscle of her body to gain that last millimetre of penetration as she felt his phallus throbbing inside her. Then she came over it in a rush of juices and an explosion of nerves, her body rigid as she sat above him, her fingers talons that clawed at his chest, raking it with her nails.

He hadn't come yet. She had felt his cock throbbing inside her but he was still hard. She slipped off him and lay on her back, pulling him down on top of her. She knew some men had to be on top, it was a kind of sexual imperative without which they could not perform. If she had been thinking, she would not have marked Paul down as that kind of chauvinist, but the last thing she was doing was thinking. She was acting instinctively, her body and the stranger she had become were in control, dictating her actions and her needs. The stranger needed Paul to come.

Paul rolled on top of her, his erection pressed between their bodies. He raised himself on one elbow and looked down into her eyes. He looked as though he wanted to say something to her, something profound, to explain something to her. Then he changed his mind and kissed her instead, a hard, needy kiss, pushing his tongue into her mouth as he bucked his hips to move his erection down between her legs.

But Nadine was in no mood for evasions.

'Say it,' she said breaking away from his mouth.

'No,' he said. It was an admission that she was right, that he was holding something back.

'Tell me,' she insisted.

'I can't.'

He drove his hips forward. After what she'd been through her sex was so slippery and open he penetrated her effortlessly, driving up into her in one fluid movement. It took her breath away. Immediately he began driving into her, pounding her as though he were trying to distract her from the conversation.

Nadine recovered from the first rush of pleasure and concentrated on Paul. She wanted to please him. For most of the evening she had not cared about his feelings but now she found she cared very much. His body was tense, his face buried in her shoulders, and she raised her head to look down his slim back, watching him pumping up and down. She had her legs spread wide and bent at the knees. He lay between them, his tight buttocks rising and falling so fast they were almost a blur.

It was too desperate she knew. He was trying too hard. He pistoned in and out of her wildly, her copious juices making squelching noises as he moved. But she knew it was not bringing him any closer to orgasm. He was sweating, beads of perspiration running off his back and he was panting with the effort too.

'Paul, Paul, what is it? What do you want?'

'It's all right,' he whispered.

'Tell me what you want?'

But quite suddenly she knew. She knew exactly what he wanted and wouldn't say. Hadn't he taken her to the club? Hadn't he shown her a graphic representation of everything he wanted? He claimed he didn't know what they were going to see but she knew he had lied.

'Stop,' Nadine said in a voice that brooked no argument. She moved her hands to his buttocks, gripping them tightly to stay their movement. There was no pause between knowing and doing, no thought of consequences. The stranger was in control and the stranger knew exactly what to do.

'It's all right,' he repeated, 'You don't have to . . .'

Thwack. The noise of flesh smacking against flesh reverberated around the bedroom. Nadine had heard a similar noise earlier in the evening. It excited her. She felt Paul's cock spasming inside her. She raised her hand again, her palm still stinging from the first blow, and slapped it down harder on his left buttock.

'Come for me Paul,' she said. The tone of her voice surprised her. She had intended it to sound gentle and caring, instead it sounded almost threatening.

'Oh yes,' he murmured.

She raised her other hand and slapped it down on his right buttock, three times in quick succession. Each blow forced his cock deep into her sex, each intrusion feeling harder and hotter than the last, as though his cock was on fire. She could feel it jerking out of control and knew he was going to come. But more than that, what she was doing – what the stranger was doing – was refuelling the fire of her own sensations too. It was thrilling, exhilarating, and incredibly sexy in a way she did not understand or want to understand. All she needed to know was that it was making her come again.

She squeezed her body around him, using every muscle she possessed to cling to the hard shaft inside her, wanting to feel it as he came. Her hands rested on his buttocks. She could feel the heat and redness she had created.

'More?' she asked.

'Oh yes . . .' he pleaded, his voice weak and broken.

The thwack of flesh on flesh echoed around the room again. She felt his cock spasm. She slapped her hand down three times on his soft flesh. His cock bucked inside her, jerking against the muscles that held it so tightly, then his whole body shook and he gushed his semen out into her, every spurt producing a tremor of feeling that made him shudder anew.

The excitement in Nadine's body could not be contained either. Instantly she crossed the line between feeling him and feeling herself and the two became the same thing, merging until his orgasm became hers. She had had no intention of doing anything else but forcing him to take his pleasure but she had tapped into some secret in her own psyche, another undreamt-of, unimagined source of sexual delight. Suddenly she felt her body churning and shuddering, her eyes squeezed closed, her fingers clawing at his buttocks as a sharp, almost painful, orgasm flooded over her. She wriggled herself on his cock, pushing it into new positions in her sex as a way of wringing out every last ounce of sensation from the rolling waves of pleasure.

Eventually Paul got off her to lay by her side. Nadine did not move. She could feel the sheet under her thighs was wet. She turned her head to look at Paul. He was staring up at the ceiling. He turned to look at her.

'You're a remarkable woman,' he said quietly.

'And you're a remarkable man.' Once again Nadine was surprised by her own reactions. In the aftermath of passion, as the stranger relinquished control, she felt not the slightest twinge of abhorrence, not the faintest hint of regret, at what she had done. She felt only a strong streak of affection for Paul.

She smiled broadly. She had, after all, managed to achieve what she would have thought previously to be the impossible: she had forgotten about John Sewell. She had been so caught up in her own feelings, the image of Sewell had not once drifted into her mind during their sex. That, she thought, was a considerable step forward in assigning Sewell to the mists of time: it represented a definite loosening of the grip he had held over her.

Before the evening began she had thought of Paul
as an amiable distraction. Now, as she lay in a puddle
of her own juices, as her body still thrilled with the
tiny aftershocks of her multiple orgasms, it appeared
he was to be more than that.

Chapter Six

What was happening to her?

She stared out over the London skyline, again unable to concentrate on her work.

The weather had broken. The two weeks of glorious summer, of sunshine and balmy nights, had turned to hard driving rain that lashed against the big windows of her office and brought a distinct chill to the air. Nadine could see the rain pouring off the nearby roofs into the gutters, some overflowing with the volume of water.

What was happening to her?

Monday morning, after the night in Paris, after the private jet and Paul's attentiveness, was bound to be an anticlimax but Nadine was suffering from more than post-adventure blues.

She had thought she was beginning to escape the spectre of Sewell, and that might be true, but she could not escape the effect he had had on her sexually. The neatly arranged pattern of her life, carefully balanced and ordered, had been destroyed. The scales of her life were totally out of balance now, the sexual side outweighing everything else.

She had never behaved in her life as she had behaved with Paul. She could not even pretend that it had been a result of alcohol. She had certainly been intoxicated but it was entirely self-induced.

Well, perhaps not entirely. The show at the club had something to do with it. But that brought her back to Sewell.

It was Sewell who had altered her sexual agenda, who had opened her to new feelings and sensations, who had thrilled and at the same time shocked her. It was Sewell who had forced her to think about sex when before she had taken it for granted.

The show at the club had affected her because Sewell had exposed the raw nerve of her libido and left it exposed. There had been no time to grow scar tissue, to climb back into her shell, to rebalance the scales to achieve equilibrium again. The spectacle of the man being whipped had burnt itself into her psyche like the pattern of a seal into newly poured sealing-wax.

Before Sewell, she knew, she would simply have got up and walked away, probably expressing her intense distaste. But now the image refused to go away. It was a clear three-dimensional image in full colour and stereo sound. It was what had made her so brazen and what, ultimately, had made her treat Paul in the way she had.

There was nothing wrong with it, she told herself. Nothing they had done was wrong. But that didn't mean it didn't disturb her. It disturbed her because she hadn't the slightest idea what she was going to do about it, how she was going to deal with it and how it would end. She wasn't even sure what she meant by 'it'. Her new sexual drive? The way sex seemed to dominate her thoughts? Or the cloudy, murky waters of what she had felt for Betty and what she had done with Paul? Or all three muddled up together?

With a great deal of effort she began to read through the papers she was supposed to be studying.

'Hi.' Barbara swung through the door of her office. 'Look at these.'

She handed Nadine three photostats of press cuttings from tabloid newspapers, all stories about the Pantie-Pads and how they were a truly revolutionary product – which, of course, they weren't. The stories represented thousands of pounds of free advertising.

'Has the client seen these?' Nadine marvelled at the way Barbara appeared to be able to get coverage on even the most mundane products.

'Of course.'

'I suppose that means you're in for another raise.'

'I bloody well hope so.'

'What do you actually do, Babs? Give them head in their offices?'

'Wouldn't you like to know? How about I buy you lunch?'

'Great. Give me thirty minutes.'

'I'll meet you there.'

There was no need to specify where. Barbara and Nadine, like many of the staff of the agency, lunched at a small Italian restaurant round the corner from the office.

Half-an-hour later Barbara was already sitting at 'their' table, toying with a tall glass of Campari and soda, when Nadine walked in. She ordered mineral water from an attractive waiter.

'Rough weekend?' Barbara commented on her choice of drink.

'Paul took me to Paris.'

Barbara laughed. 'That's what I like about you, darling. Such a slow worker. I take it you acquiesced to his wicked desires?'

'You're so subtle, Babs.'

'And?'

Nadine had no intention of telling her friend the details of what had happened but was glad to spill some of the beans.

'I told him sex was out of the question.'

'And he accepted that?'

The waiter arrived to take their order. They always ate the same thing, Barbara a plate of *insalata tricoloure* and Nadine *pollo milanese*. Both ordered a single glass of red wine.

'So?' Barabara prodded when the waiter had gone. 'You didn't sleep with him?'

'I did. I changed my mind.'

'And did the earth move?'

'As a matter of face the earth felt like it had been hit by a giant meteor.'

'Really? The sly dog. I never knew he had it in him. So when's the next cosmic collision?'

'He's taking me out to dinner on Wednesday.'

'You don't sound very happy about it.'

'He's a nice man, I think.'

'You think?'

'You've known him longer than I have. You tell me.'

'Oh, I don't know him *that* well. I met him at some

174

press do. He's a spare man to invite to dinner parties, you know how handy that is.'

'Oh thanks.'

'Don't mention it. He's divorced, I know that.'

'He told me.'

'But he didn't tell you why?'

'No. That would be interesting. I'll put that on the agenda for Wednesday night.'

'I get the feeling you're holding out on me.'

'Would I do such a thing?'

'So, what's that problem?'

'I'm not sure there is one.'

'Oh yes, there is.'

'I'll tell you Thursday.'

'Intriguing.' Barbara left it at that. They had been friends a long time and she knew when not to trespass onto the private and sensitive areas. Barbara would always be there to listen whenever Nadine wanted to tell her more.

Nadine had slept like the dead on Monday night, a deep and apparently dreamless slumber, waking up in the same position as she had gone to sleep and feeling wonderfully refreshed. Perhaps her subconscious had worked away at her worries, played them all out in dreams as a way of resolving them, then tactfully drawn a curtain over the whole episode so she couldn't remember a thing. Whatever had been going on during the night she certainly felt more at ease and less stressed than she had on Monday.

Work, too, served to take her mind from endless

unproductive mulling-over of recent events. From the moment she got into the office, her phone never stopped ringing. The Brandling Corporation had delayed the decision on who to appoint as their new advertising agency but Nadine had heard they were definitely leaning towards her presentation. She should, she supposed, have called John Sewell and told him the news as a matter of politeness but he was the one person she did not want to talk to.

But Brandling was not her only concern. The storyboard for the new Pantie-Pad commercial had gone to the client who, having approved the campaign at the concept stage, had now decided they wanted to scrap the whole approach – though of course they still wanted to launch the product on the same date. That involved conceiving, plotting and shooting an entirely new commercial in a two-week time span.

This led Nadine to an endless round of telephone calls and frantically arranged meetings to get a series of ideas to put to the client by Friday, which was the absolute deadline for making decisions, if, by the skin of their teeth, a new commercial was to be made in time.

It was eight o'clock in the evening when Nadine finally got home, satisfied she had done everything she could to ensure the client got what they wanted but did not deserve.

Kicking off her shoes and stripping herself out of her clothes, she ran a bath and lay in the tub for a long time, allowing the tensions of the day to soak away, helped by a large gin and tonic. She ran more hot water into the bath to prevent the water getting too cold but eventually, and reluctantly, as her flesh began to pucker like a dried fruit, she pulled herself out of the water and wrapped herself in a white towelling robe that she had once liberated from a five-star hotel bedroom.

It was as she dried her hair and began to think about what to eat that her doorbell rang.

She looked at her watch. She wasn't expecting any visitors and had no desire to see anyone. She hoped it wasn't Paul. She was happy to see him tomorrow but tonight she was too tired to make the necessary effort.

She opened the front door a crack, leaving the security chain on.

'Hi, Nadine.'

Nadine couldn't have been more surprised if she'd opened the door to Santa Claus. Standing with a bottle of wine under her arm, the collar of a grey raincoat turned up around her neck against the drizzling rain, was Betty Holden.

As she closed the door to release the chain Nadine felt her pulse racing. She opened the door fully not at all sure what she was going to say.

'May I come in?' Betty asked tentatively, seeing the shock in Nadine's face.

'Yes ... yes ...' She could hardly say no, though that might well have been her first reaction. She stood aside then closed the door as Betty walked into the hall.

'This is for you.' Betty handed her the bottle of wine. It was an expensive Burgundy.

'There's no need . . .' Nadine said, still floundering for something to say, as well as an attitude to strike. Betty stood awkwardly shifting from one foot to the other, waiting for Nadine to show her into the house, or tell her she wanted her to leave. The silence was heavy with implication.

'Sorry,' Nadine said decisively, finally making her own mind up. 'Come through.'

'Look, if you'd rather . . .' Betty's voice trailed away, not wanting to give Nadine too much opportunity to change her mind.

'No. Now you're here, come in.' She sounded more definite than she felt.

Betty followed her into the living room.

'This is nice.'

'Would you like a drink?'

'Please.'

'We'll share the bottle.' Nadine said holding up the Burgundy. Sharing a bottle implied a longer time frame than a single drink, of course, but the flood of emotion she had felt at seeing Betty again had stabilised and she was curious to know why Betty was here. There were a few questions of her own she would like answered.

'Make yourself at home. I'll get some glasses.'

Betty was wearing a short white top over shiny black leggings. She wore spiky black high heels in an effort, no doubt, to increase her height, and she was carrying a big black handbag slung over her shoulder. She sat on one of the two sofas that faced each other in the living room.

Nadine took the bottle out into the kitchen and

used the levered corkscrew to open it, giving herself time to think. Had Sewell sent Betty here to entice Nadine back into their bed of crimson joy? It seemed the most likely explanation and the one for which she would have the simplest of answers. She took two glasses from a cupboard, wrapped the robe more tightly around her body and walked back into the living room. As she put the glasses on the coffee table between the sofas and poured the wine she was aware of Betty watching her intently. She handed Betty a glass and sat on the sofa opposite, tucking her legs up underneath her.

'Did Sewell send you?' Nadine said firmly.

'God no. He has no idea I'm here.'

'Why are you here then?' There was no point beating around the bush.

Betty paused for a moment before answering. 'If you want the truth I'm not entirely sure myself. It seemed like a good idea at the time.'

'There must be a reason.' Nadine was in no mood for equivocation.

'Oh, there's lots of reasons. I'm not sure which makes the most sense. Sewell never stops talking about you.'

'The one that got away.'

'Sorry?'

'He talks about me because I wouldn't take his calls, because I frustrated his plans, whatever they were.'

'He wanted to paint you.'

'It seems to me, painting and sex are inextricably linked as far as Sewell is concerned.'

'True.'

'I don't want to get involved with him again.'

'Why not?'

Nadine paused wanting to give an accurate answer, as much for herself as Betty. 'Because sex to me isn't a game.'

'Is that what you thought?'

'Yes. I thought he was . . .' she corrected herself, 'I thought you were playing a very dangerous game.'

'I can understand that.'

'Good. So did you come here to try and persuade me back?'

'Yes and no.'

'Explain.'

'Sewell would kill me if he found out I was going to tell you this.'

'What?'

'I think he's in love with you.'

'Love!' The word astonished Nadine.

'I've never known him get into such a depression. He's not working. He's drinking too much. All since that night. He's pining for you, Nadine, that's the truth though I doubt he'd admit it. He wants you.'

'Sexually maybe.'

'I think it's more than that.'

'What makes you think that?'

'I just know.'

'What about you?'

'He's not in love with me. He never has been.'

'Why do you stay then?'

'Because I get the best of all possible worlds.'

'I don't understand.'

'Men and women. I like both. And Sewell is a great provider.'

Nadine hoped her astonishment didn't show on her face. She sipped her wine.

'I like . . .' Betty continued, 'what did you call them? Dangerous games.'

'And do you like Sewell?'

'I love Sewell. I'm mad about him. He's wonderful. If he wanted me to be mono-sexual – is there such a word? – I'd probably agree. But he never has. I always knew the day would come when I'd have to step aside.'

'For me?' Nadine couldn't help her voice rising an octave. She felt her pulse racing again. Just as it seemed she had managed to sideline Sewell and escape from those dark hypnotic eyes, she saw them looking at her again. She found it hard to believe what Betty was saying.

'Are you sure Sewell didn't send you?'

'He's too proud. He called you several times, didn't he? And you never replied. That's so out of character for him. He's normally the sort of man who'd freeze to death before he'd ask anyone for a lump of coal.'

'So what's in it for you?' The sentence came out rather more harshly than Nadine had intended.

Betty drank some wine. 'Nothing. I just thought you should know, that's all.'

It clearly wasn't all. There was something Betty was not saying.

'Altruism?'

'I think Sewell is special, I'd like to see him happy.'

'He's happy isn't he? Christ he's got what most men only dream about.'

'I don't think he's really happy.'

'Perhaps he'll never be happy.'

'He could be. With the right woman.'

'Really?' Nadine sounded sceptical. 'You mean you think he's capable of monogamy?'

'Yes.'

Nadine thought about this for a moment, recalling the way she had felt about Sewell before she had discovered Betty's things.

'And you're saying you think I'm the right woman?'

'Definitely, from the way he talks about you. He's smitten. He's never been smitten before. Women have always thrown themselves at him. He's never reciprocated before.'

Betty was looking at Nadine, as though she were trying to judge whether she should go on. She put her wine glass down on the coffee table next to a pile of *Campaign* magazines that had accumulated over the weeks.

'That's not the only reason I came.'

'Go on,' Nadine said calmly, not feeling calm at all.

'No. Actually I think I've made a mistake.'

'A mistake?'

'Yes.'

'About what?'

Betty smiled. Nadine noticed she had very regular, very white teeth. Her face was beautiful, small-featured but distinctive, dominated by her brown eyes and fleshy mouth. Nadine had noticed it in the mirror in Sewell's bedroom and in the painting of the mirror; she remembered the way the lines of ecstasy had been etched on its contours. A frisson of pleasure ran through her body.

'About you. About us. Forget it. I've said what I came to say. It's up to you now, if you want to do anything about it.'

'What do you mean about us?' Nadine didn't want that subject to be dropped.

'I didn't mean to say that.'

'Yes, you did.' Nadine had seen something in Betty's brown eyes, something that excited her. A few weeks ago, even if it had occurred to her at all, which would have been highly unlikely, she would have dismissed it. Now she couldn't do that. It was something she wanted to explore almost despite herself.

'Look, Nadine . . .' Betty tried to think of a way of getting herself off the hook. She couldn't. She stood up. 'All right, if you really must know I came to tell you about Sewell. But I also thought, well felt, there was something between us. I wanted you. I wanted to have sex with you again. Now I'd better go, I'm sorry, I know it's not what you wanted to hear.'

An icy calm descended on Nadine. She had known that was what Betty was going to say, long before she had spoken the words. For some reason she did not understand it had been obvious. Her reaction was equally straightforward.

'I don't want you to go,' she said getting to her feet, feeling a kick of excitement hit her in the stomach. Half of her mind – or was it less than half? – was wondering what the hell she thought she was doing. The other half knew. She was following her instincts, listening to her body, to the rhythms and cadences of her sex which now played so loudly and so close to the surface. She didn't want to think about implications and consequences. The stranger was in control again.

Betty looked at her steadily. Even with her heels on she was shorter than Nadine and had to tilt her head to look into her face.

'What then?' she asked quietly.

'Tell me what you were going to say. You must have worked it out.'

She filled Betty's wine glass and her own and sat down again in the corner of the sofa. Betty sat on the same sofa this time, in the opposite corner. There was clear space between them.

'I was going to say . . .' She hesitated.

'Go on.'

'If you want the truth, I was going to say that I found you an incredibly sexy and desirable woman and I really wanted to take you to bed again. After that, I sort of hoped we'd just fall into each other's arms.'

The stranger was in control again. Nadine extended her arm along the back of the sofa until her fingers reached Betty's cheek. She stroked it with the back of her hand. She had never felt the slightest desire for a woman before, never wanted to have sex with a woman or even imagined what it would be like, but she was doing and feeling all those things now. She was surprised her hand wasn't trembling. Her desire was like a hard knot being pulled constantly tighter in the pit of her stomach.

Betty turned her head to the side and brushed her lips against Nadine's finger. She looked straight into her eyes. Betty's expression was easy to read. It said, 'Are you sure?'

Nadine answered the unasked question by moving her hand around to Betty's neck and pulling her into a kiss, squirming her lips against her mouth, using her tongue to explore inside, feeling Betty's tongue eager to take its turn at penetration. The kiss was hot and passionate, more passionate that Nadine would have thought possible. It was all so sudden, it was as though a dam had burst and emotion flooded out through the breached walls. But Nadine had not known the dam was there, let alone the lake of feelings swollen up behind it.

There was nothing hesitant about what she did. She felt Betty's hands caressing her back and wrapped her arms around her in turn, until the two were locked in an embrace. Everything in her life had changed. As she felt the waves of sensation coursing through her body, as she registered a physical need as strong as she had felt for any man, she realised she was about to go to bed with a woman, have sex with a woman, for the first time. Of course, that wasn't strictly true. She had been in Betty's arms before. But that had been at Sewell's behest, it had been for him, part of the sexual symphony he had orchestrated. This was entirely different. Nadine could not pretend she was doing this for any other reason but for herself, to satisfy her own desire.

Betty broke the kiss and pulled back.

'You don't mess about, do you?' she said smiling.

'You were right. I didn't know it, but you were right.'

'Where's the bedroom?'

'First door on the right at the top of the stairs.'

'Give me a couple of minutes,' Betty said getting to her feet, picking up her handbag and walking out of the living-room door. Nadine could hear her footsteps going up the stairs and along the landing. She listened as she heard the bathroom door open and close and the toilet flush.

She could have stopped it there but she didn't think about doing that for a single second. The feel of Betty's mouth and body, the smell of her scent, the touch of her hands had revived memories in Nadine's body that were far too strong to ignore. She knew she had deliberately suppressed a lot of feelings Betty had aroused in her that night with Sewell. She'd transferred them to him, made him the author of everything that had happened, not wanting to face the fact that her pleasure with Betty had been a thing apart.

But it had. She felt stronger now. If having a woman was part of her long neglected sexual make-up she wanted to know it. She wanted to know precisely what it was that made her tick. Over the past weeks she had received untold-of pleasures from her own body and she had no intention of going back to the good-old bad-old days when sex had been something like a household chore. She wanted all the details because she wanted to learn about her needs. Sex was an undiscovered country for her.

Well, having set foot on its shores she was determined she was going to explore it, map it out in detail, find out all the secret landscapes and hidden byways. There was nothing to fear any more.

She finished her glass of wine and stood up. There was a gilt-framed mirror over the reproduction Adam fireplace and she looked at her face closely. Her eyes were sparkling, dancing with the flame her excitement had fuelled.

She walked upstairs remarkably calmly. Her bedroom door was ajar. She pushed it open. The light in the room had been dimmed to a rosy glow because Betty had draped a towel over the bedside lamp on one side of the bed. She had also stripped away the bedding and was lying naked on the bottom sheet, her head propped up against the pillows, her fingers wrapped around two of the brass stanchions, stretching her arms wide apart. Her legs were spread apart too, her big breasts lolling on her chest, their nipples stiff and puckered.

Nadine stood by the side of the bed.

'You have a beautiful body,' she said. Betty's flesh had a sheen to it like the finest silk. Nadine stretched out her hand to touch her leg.

'Thank you, but I'm too short and my breasts are too big.'

Nadine stroked the top of her leg from her knee to her thigh. She was in no hurry now. She had made her decision, if that's what it was. It didn't feel as though she had decided anything. Her body had led her on.

'You're so soft,' Nadine said.

187

'Do you like that?'

'Mmm . . .'

'Women are so different from men.' Betty was watching Nadine's hand as it stroked her flesh. 'Not just the obvious differences. All sorts of other things.'

Nadine moved her hand to Betty's belly. It was not quite flat, there was a suggestion of rotundity, a slight plumpness that was reflected in the lips of her sex. The side of Nadine's hand grazed her thick black pubic hair. Still with no sense of urgency she moved her hand up to Betty's breast, gathering it in until her fingers were full of the spongy pliant flesh. She squeezed it then rolled the nipple between her fingers. What was happening to her? What was she doing? She felt excitement oozing out of her body like sweat.

She was hot. She let go of Betty's breast and, unselfconsciously stripped off her robe.

'You have a beautiful body,' Betty echoed, smiling.

Nadine did not reply. She got up onto the bed and lay down beside Betty, facing her. Betty turned her head and they looked into each other's eyes, their faces only inches apart.

'I've never done this before,' Nadine said. 'I mean with anyone else.'

'I know.'

'It feels different without Sewell.'

'It is.'

'Will you help me?'

'I don't think you'll need much help. Just do whatever you want.'

Betty lifted her hand to stroke Nadine's cheek,

then, moving closer, kissed her forehead and cheeks, and then her mouth, little nibbling kisses. She wrapped her arms around Nadine and pressed her body against hers.

'That feels so good . . .' Nadine said.

Their breasts joined together. Nadine could feel Betty's belly and her curly pubic hair pressing hard against her navel. She had never felt this before, a naked woman lying against her, the softness of a woman's body – so different from a man's. She felt a surge of desire like an electric shock, sharp and energising. She rolled Betty over onto her back and moved on top of her. This is what a man must feel she thought, dominant and powerful. Betty's legs slipped open and Nadine's left thigh fell between them. She pushed it upward immediately and felt Betty's sex against her flesh. It was hot and wet.

'What should I do?' she whispered.

'That, just do that . . .'

She felt Betty wriggling herself against her thigh, shifting her sex from side to side, so her clitoris was squeezed one way and then the other. She thought she could actually feel it, swollen and hard, moving against her flesh but it was probably only her fevered imagination.

'My handbag . . .' Betty mumbled. She had put it on the bedside table. Puzzled, Nadine managed to reach the strap without changing her position. She pulled it onto the bed and Betty delved inside. 'Use this,' she said, her voice husky and deep.

She had produced a black plastic phallus from her bag. It was thick and long, with ribbed indentations

189

along most of its length. Its tip was crudely shaped to resemble the glans of a penis. Betty thrust it into Nadine's hand.

Nadine's feelings stirred again, another wave of excitement flooding over her. She grasped the dildo firmly, remembering what it was like to thrust one up into her own body. Now she had the means to deliver the same pleasure to Betty.

Nadine slipped off Betty's body and knelt besides her on the bed. She turned the knob at the base of the phallus and felt it spring to life in her hand, the familiar humming filling the air. She trailed the tip over Betty's breast up to her left nipple, then across to the right. Betty moaned slightly and closed her eyes. Nadine slipped the dildo down over her belly.

'Oh that's so nice,' Betty said spreading her legs further apart. She opened her eyes to look up at Nadine. 'Do you use a dildo?' she asked.

'I have, recently . . .'

'I love them, I love the feeling of having something thrust up into me.'

Nadine slid the dildo down between Betty's thick puffy labia, watching with fascination as the black plastic buried itself in the furrow of her sex. Betty's nether lips seemed to be kissing it, drawing it in, sucking it up.

'Love it . . .' Betty said.

Nadine turned the knob again to increase the intensity of the vibration. Betty gasped.

'Right on your clit,' Nadine said. Even through the thick dark hair, she could see it, a little pink promontory nestling in a valley of flesh. She pushed the vibrating tip of the dildo right up against it and saw Betty squirm. But the vibration was getting to her too, spreading through her body from her hand to her sex, as though there were some direct connection between the two.

Betty raised her hands and cupped both her big breasts. To Nadine's amazement she began feeding the nipple of her left breast into her mouth, baring her lips so Nadine could see she was holding the puckered flesh between her teeth.

The hum of the vibrator was relentless. Betty's body tensed. Nadine could see the tendons pulled taut by her passion. She threw her head back, her nipple still firmly clenched between her teeth, stretching her breasts to the limit, until her teeth lost their grip and the pink flesh quivered. With a visible effort, Betty reached down to repeat the process with her other breast, taking the nipple between her teeth then stretching her head backward until her breast was pulled taut and the pleasure of the pain from her nipple took her to the brink of orgasm. Then the thread broke, the breast sprung back and Betty was pitched over the edge.

'Now,' she cried, hoping Nadine would know what she meant. She did. As she saw Betty's body arch off the bed she thrust the dildo up into her sex. There was no resistance, it plunged forward on a tide of Betty's juices, squelching against the silky inner walls. Nadine turned the knob to its maximum and heard the note of the vibrator change.

She began pumping it in and out of Betty's vagina, imitating the action of a real cock, watching with total fascination as the dildo emerged glistening with Betty's juices, before it was almost completely engulfed in the voracious mouth of the other woman's sex.

'Yes, yes, yes,' Betty cried loudly.

Suddenly her hand shot out and grabbed Nadine's wrist. It was as though her fingers were made of steel. She held her tight, so the dildo was buried in her body and Nadine could not withdraw it again. Betty's own wrist bore down on her clitoris, the strap of her watch biting into it.

'Yes,' she shouted again as her orgasm was prolonged, every nerve in her body responding to the pounding vibration that emanated from deep inside her sex, her grip on Nadine's wrist ensuring that the dildo remained buried deep within her.

Slowly the orgasm faded. Nadine felt the tension slacken, saw her eyes open and the ring of steel on her wrist relaxed.

Betty pulled her hand away from the base of the dildo. The folds of her sex slowly expelled the intruder and, as the dildo fell on to the sheet between her legs, she shuddered again.

Betty sat up and turned off the dildo.

'Now it's your turn, darling,' Betty said, smiling a knowing, secret smile – a smile that said she was about to introduce Nadine into a conspiracy. 'You've only used one on yourself, right? It feels so much better with someone else.'

'It felt good doing it to you.'

'Lie back.'

Nadine obeyed immediately. Her body was already

aching with need. What she had done to Betty and the way it had looked had turned her on. The vibration from the phallus in her hand still echoed throughout her body.

Betty got up onto her knees. Taking the dildo in her left hand, she gathered Nadine's breast in her right and squeezed it so the nipple was forced out between her fingers. She turned the dildo on and applied the tip to the nipple. Nadine felt it pucker despite the fact it was already stiff. Betty used the same technique on the other breast, then trailed the dildo down over Nadine's navel. It was still wet and a slick trail of sex juice marked its passage.

Nadine's legs were spread though she could not remember opening them. The tip of the dildo slid into the triangle of short pubic hair pointing downwards to the apex of her thighs, like a large arrow. She felt the vibrations beginning to affect her clitoris.

'Is that good?' Betty asked.

'Yes.'

'And this?'

Though Nadine had used the dildo on herself, it hadn't felt anything like this. As the tip of the dildo slid onto the little nut of her clitoris she felt as though she had stopped breathing, as though the world had ceased to exist except for the electric thrill that shook her body, so extreme it felt as though it was turning her inside out.

In seconds, less than seconds, her sex nerves were stretched taut and she was on fire, just as Betty had been. She grabbed the rails of the brass bedstead and tossed her head from side to side, every sense concentrated on that tiny spot between her legs that was making her come.

'Oh Christ . . .' she screamed, the vibration of the words against the walls of the room somehow matching the vibration of her body. Then she was falling, her orgasm so sudden she barely had time to realise it was happening, there was no gap between the realisation and the response.

But it didn't end there. As Nadine's eyes were forced closed by the impact of what was happening to her, she felt the dildo move. With her body still trembling from the effects of one orgasm, the vibrator was plunged all the way up her vagina, the juices of her body making the passage effortless, the hard phallus filling her completely.

Though she had just come, she knew she was coming again, one orgasm climbing on the back of the other. There was so much sensation, she felt so much pleasure she thought she might faint. Every part of her sex seemed alive. She could feel it throbbing and pulsing, as her nerves, like a swelling crescendo of violins, all joined to play the same tune. Every part of her body, from the joints of her fingers to the back of her knees to the sinews of her neck, wanting to play a part.

The incredible orgasm went on so long that when she opened her eyes again she had to blink against the brightness of the light.

Betty was looking down at her, still holding the dildo in her body though she had turned it off.

'Now this,' she said letting go of the base. Nadine

felt her body closing, the cavern of her sex folding itself together again as, with seemingly infinite slowness, she felt the dildo slide out. Nadine gasped as an echo of all the sensations she had experienced shuddered through her body.

'That was wonderful,' she said, sitting up. She took Betty's face between both her hands and kissed her full on the mouth, plunging her tongue between her lips. Betty's mouth was much hotter than it had been before, and wetter too, as though what had happened in her sex was repeated there.

'Betty, Betty . . .' she said with their mouths still joined so the words were barely audible. Nadine didn't want it to end there. Almost before she knew what she was doing she was pushing Betty back onto the bed with an urgency that belied what she had just experienced.

'What have you done to me?' she said. There was no hesitancy now, or reluctance. She knew exactly what she wanted and how to get it. She was taking the lead, making the running. As soon as Betty was lying flat she swung her thigh over her shoulders so her sex was poised above Betty's mouth. She had the strangest sensation. It felt as though her sex was articulate, as though she could use it as she used her mouth – smile with it, kiss with it, suck with it.

Betty had spread her legs and bent her knees. Nadine looked down at her, the black pubic hair plastered back by all the wetness, exposing her labia and the scarlet, crinkled slit of her sex. With the fingers of one hand Nadine spread the labia apart wanting to see Betty's clitoris again. It pulsed visibly. She felt her own body throb too, as though in response. She loved this, she loved the feelings Betty had given her, she loved each and every sensation. The truth was she loved sex.

Running her hands under Betty's thighs she dipped her head to taste the other woman's sex in her mouth again, at the same time lowering her hungry vagina onto Betty's waiting lips.

Chapter Seven

It was a beautiful house. She didn't think she had ever been in a house so immaculately decorated nor so extravagantly furnished – and in perfect taste. Though it was obvious no expense had been spared, there was nothing flashy or ostentatious in the way it had been done. It had the air of an English country house: heavy curtains, chunky sofas, leather armchairs, rugs laid on wooden floors and shelves upon shelves of books. Anything redolent of the twentieth century – television, hi-fi – was hidden out of sight.

The Rolls Royce had arrived to pick her up at eight as arranged. Paul had called her from the plane to say his flight from Milan had been delayed and he was going to send Vernon to bring her to the house, by which time he should have arrived from the airport.

In fact, the Rolls had pulled up in Nash Terrace, where his house was located, just as a black cab dropped him off.

He showed her the house and opened a bottle of Krug Grande Cuvée. The living room led onto a small but private garden and he had opened the large french windows to let in a breath of fresh air. After the rain of the past two days the sun had emerged and the scent of summer flowers drying out in the heat wafted in from the carefully planted garden.

'Look, I must shower and change,' he said. 'I've been in the same clothes all day. Then we'll go out and eat. I am sorry about this. Commercial flights are never on time.'

'Don't worry, take your time,' Nadine said, waving him away, though he seemed reluctant to leave her.

'I won't be long.'

'Go then,' she said.

'Help yourself to champagne.'

'Go . . .'

Left alone, Nadine wandered around the room, sipping the champagne from a crystal flute and admiring the *objets d'art* that littered every surface and the paintings on the walls, all individually lit and carefully sited.

She had no intention of going out to dinner with Paul but she thought better not to tell him that just yet. It was only fair that she allowed him to shower and change. She knew how it felt to be travel weary.

But after that she would tell him. There was only one thing she wanted from Paul tonight and she wanted it badly, as badly as she had ever wanted anything.

She had dressed accordingly. Two years ago she had brought, entirely on a whim, in a Bond Street sale, a catsuit in a shiny glass-effect black Lycra. She had never worn it – she had never dared. It was so tight and so clinging it followed every contour of her body, revealing the roundness of her breasts and the buttons of her nipples, shaping itself to her body so perfectly it buried itself in the furrow of her sex and the deep cleft of her buttocks. She had never found an occasion to wear it until now. Tonight she had squeezed into it and used a pair of black high-heeled ankle boots to shape and firm the muscles of her legs and buttocks, emphasising the taut curves of her bottom most of all.

She looked like a whore, an expensive and exclusive whore maybe, but a whore nonetheless. It was exactly the impression she wanted to give.

She glanced at her watch, took a sip of the champagne, put the glass down and decided not to wait for Paul.

Nadine mounted the stairs. At the top she heard the sound of water running and headed in that direction. The door to what was obviously the master bedroom was open. She walked in, went to the large windows overlooking Regent's Park and drew the curtains, plunging the room into a dim twilight.

The room was large. The double bed was almost twice the normal width. There were no wardrobes or chests of drawers, just a small sofa and two large comfortable armchairs. Tall brass lamps stood on walnut bedside tables on either side of the bed, their green shades toning with the rest of the decor.

There were three doors along one wall which at first she took to be built-in wardrobes. They were constructed to be flush and with the wall with no architrave. But when she opened the first she discovered it led to a narrow dressing room racked with shelves and rails from which hung a large collection of Paul's clothes. The second door was locked. The third opened onto the bathroom, also a long narrow room, but this time decorated in the finest marble, a white and grey striation with hints of black.

The shower stall was a separate cubicle at the far end. It had misted up with steam.

Nadine walked the length of the room, her high heels clacking on the marble floor. She could feel her pulse rate rise.

She had never behaved like this before in her life. How many times had she said that to herself in the last few weeks? The stranger was in control again but this time, unlike in Paris and with Betty, she knew the stranger a great deal better. Before she could pretend the stranger who made her do these things was not her at all but was some anomaly, a creation of her libido. Now she knew the stranger only too well, so well it was almost as if her old self, the one with little sex drive, the one who had never seduced a man or gone to bed with a woman, was the real stranger.

She didn't want to think about it. She didn't want to think about anything. She just wanted sex.

'Paul . . .' She opened the shower cubicle door. Paul stood naked in a stream of water, steam filling the small space. He turned to look at her as she pulled down the zip of the catsuit. It ran from her neck to her crotch. She kicked off the boots and peeled away the clinging Lycra. She wasn't wearing anything else.

He moved his hand to turn off the water.

'No,' she said. 'Leave it on.'

She climbed in beside him and closed the shower

door behind her. Warm water cascaded off her body as she wrapped her arms around him and kissed him hard on the lips, pushing her belly against his, feeling his cock beginning to swell.

'I want you,' she said breaking the kiss, water running down her face, her hair plastered to her head.

'You're wonderful,' he said.

'Don't say anything, Paul, just do it.'

He kissed her shoulders and her breasts, water pouring off her body as the powerful shower gushed over them. She dropped to her knees, pulled back the foreskin of his cock, then sunk her mouth over it, sucking hard. She felt him growing, getting bigger all the time.

Nadine was in no mood for finesse. As soon as he was hard she pushed him back against the marble wall and climbed onto his body, throwing her arms around his neck and hoisting herself up until his cock thrust between her legs. She knew she was wet – she had been wet in the back of the Rolls, thinking about what she was going to do – but the water had a drying effect, washing away her natural slipperiness and sealing her vagina. She took his cock in her hand and pushed herself down on it. For a moment nothing happened. She delved between her labia and plunged a finger inside herself, breaking the seal. Beyond she was hot and creamy. Immediately she guided his cock to the opening she had made and pushed down on him again. This time he slid past the initial barrier. Beyond, he wallowed in a sea of silky wet. She ground down on him and he was propelled deeper.

'Yes, that's what I need,' she said triumphantly.

She bucked against him, pressing her round, firm breasts against his chest, kissing him fiercely on the mouth. He thrust up into her strongly but the penetration in this position was not deep enough.

Nadine broke away, pulling the shower door open and taking Paul by the hand. They ran into the bedroom, their wet feet making footprints on the thick bedroom carpet, and threw themselves onto the bed, rolling over until Nadine was on her back and Paul was on top.

He thrust into her again immediately. His cock felt bigger than it had in Paris and harder.

'Is this . . . what . . . you want?' he said between strokes.

'Don't talk.'

She didn't want to hear his voice. She didn't want to see him. She just wanted cock – hard, horny cock. Sewell's cock. If the truth were known it was Sewell she wanted, Sewell inside her, Sewell on top of her. It was Sewell who had filled her mind since Betty's visit, images of Sewell she had tried to suppress. She wanted the hardness of his body and its beauty. She remembered it in every detail, the muscles firm and well defined, the lock of hair falling over his forehead – and his sex, throbbing and erect, the swollen plum of his glans smooth and glistening. Most of all she could see his eyes looking at her, challenging her, wanting her to come.

'Oh Christ,' she cried loudly as she came, the image of Sewell so strong it was all she could do not to call his name. She writhed and wriggled and squirmed against the cock inside her, grinding her clitoris against its base, wanting to extract every last ounce of feeling, every shock of sensation, until she had wiped away the spectre that haunted her.

It was a long time before she opened her eyes again. Paul was lying beside her, propped up on one elbow, a worried expression on his face.

'Are you all right?'

The image of Sewell had been so strong she was almost surprised to see him.

'Fine.'

'I think you needed that.'

'I did.'

'Can I ask why?'

'Women are allowed to want sex too, aren't they?'

'Yes . . .'

'I wanted you that's all,' she lied.

She could feel his erection nestling against her hip. He hadn't come. Her guilt at using him in the way she had began to surface. She moved herself against him.

'I've had what I want, so it's your turn,' she said smiling.

A shadow crossed his face, like a cloud passing over the sun. She could not read what it meant. 'What do you want, Paul?'

'Lots of things.'

'Name one.'

'It's not necessary, Nadine, really.'

'Yes it is. I want to please you.'

As he had done in Paris he looked as though he

was about to say something then changed his mind.

'Say it,' she insisted this time. Did he want a repeat of what she had done to him in Paris?

He got up off the bed and walked over to the dressing room, disappearing inside for no more than a few seconds. When he returned he was holding something in his hand.

'Put this on,' he said in a strange, flat voice, his eyes not looking into hers.

'What is it?'

But when he handed it to her it was perfectly obvious what it was. Made from padded black silk, with tight elasticated strings to hold it in place, it was a sleeping mask, shaped to fit neatly around her eyes and nose so no light would filter through.

Why Paul wanted her to be blindfolded she had no idea. She could have asked him, of course, but didn't want to. She had used him and it was only fair he got the chance to use her.

She slipped the mask over her face and arranged it over her eyes. It was a tight fit and she was immediately plunged into total darkness. The strange thing was that the darkness created a surge of excitement, the tendrils of her orgasm suddenly springing back to life. After Paris, she knew Paul's sexuality was far from straightforward but she hadn't expected this.

She felt his hands on her shoulders laying her gently back on the bed. There was a peculiar sense of anonymity behind the mask, as though she was no longer an individual, as though it didn't matter what she thought. Was that the *raison d'être*?

Nadine felt Paul moving. She heard one of the drawers in the bedside table opening and felt Paul's weight shift as he came up onto his knees besides her. With nothing to see, sound and smell became magnified. She thought she could smell leather and hear a rustling as though Paul was attaching something to his body.

She started when his hand touched her breast. His fingers centred on her nipples and pinched them both in turn, hard enough to evoke the pleasure of pain. She felt him moving up the bed and then his erection pushed forward, nudging into the soft meat of her breast until she could feel his glans against her nipple. He began moving it to and fro, the whole shaft pressed into her. She could feel his balls and thought she could feel something hard underneath them, a tight leather strap perhaps.

He had one hand on her belly and the other on top of his cock. Then she felt him move the hand on her breast away, though the rhythm of his cock pressing into her pliant flesh and the hard puckered nipple did not stop. He leant back slightly then forward again and Nadine felt a trickle of wet pouring over his erection and down over her breast, enveloping it in a slippery, thick oil.

With his other hand he massaged the oil all over both breasts, the one he was pumping and the other one, then his hand trailed down to her belly again. Her legs were open and he had no trouble sliding a well-oiled finger between her labia and onto her clitoris.

In the darkness behind the mask her clitoris

seemed extra sensitive. His finger pressed it down against her pubic bone while his other hand pushed his cock into the soft flesh of her breast. In the same tempo as he was using with his cock, his finger circled her clit.

Nadine moaned, a long continuous sound. She was surprised at how being deprived of one sense seemed to accentuate the others. Her sensitivity to touch had increased to a fever pitch in seconds. Her whole body shuddered. She knew now he was going to come on her breast, shoot his hot seed all over her, and the idea excited her almost as much as the careful ministrations of his finger.

She could feel his cock tense and throb urgently, her own body responding with just as much enthusiasm. Though she could see nothing, in her mind the image of his cock pressing hard into her soft breast and nudging against her nipple was vivid, propelling her to her own orgasm.

Paul stopped, the slit of his urethra against her nipple. Nadine felt him pushing his erection down into her breast and then his cock began to spasm. Instantly she felt a sticky liquid jetting out over her, spraying all over her chest and throat, its heat intense.

Again the darkness helped. She saw it all in her mind, hot white semen gushing over her, the ecstasy etched on Paul's face, his body stretched and taut. As his finger started moving on her clitoris again her body responded instantly. A great shock of sensation surged through her and, in the blackness that engulfed her, she saw scarlet and crimson light exploding as she arched herself up off the bed. She came on a wave of pure excitement at what had been done to her and what it had made her feel.

'Hello?' His voice was as rich as she remembered, like dark chocolate mousse.

'Hi,' she said trying to sound casual and cheery. 'It's Nadine.'

The voice on the other end of the line brightened immediately. 'This is a pleasant surprise.'

'I wanted to tell you about the Brandling account. They've delayed the decision.'

'Oh.' He sounded disappointed.

'I'm sure we'll get it though. I've a friend on the inside. She says we're a sure thing. They've just got some budget problems that have got to be sorted out first.'

'I see. Is that the only reason you're calling?'

'Yes. No. I want to see you, Sewell.' She hadn't worked out what she was going to say to him beforehand. She wished she hadn't mentioned Brandling.

'I'd like that. Why don't you come round?'

'No,' Nadine said very definitely.

'What then?'

'Why don't you come to me. Dinner tomorrow?'

'Friday. That's great.'

'Eight?'

'I'll be there.'

There was a pause.

'What is it?' he asked.

'It's good to hear your voice,' she said before

she had a chance to stop herself.

'I'm glad you rang, Nadine. Very.' That sounded genuine.

Nadine put the phone down. She went back into her living room and curled up on the sofa, taking a sip of the red wine she had left on the coffee table.

She had done it. It had taken her all day and most of the evening to pluck up the courage but she had finally done it. Her heart was still pounding and her hand was trembling. He had sounded pleased to hear from her. It looked as if Betty was right.

Nadine rested her head on the back of the sofa and closed her eyes. She was behaving like a teenage girl with a crush. She tried to calm herself down, telling herself not to be so silly. Her moods and emotions had suffered several swings since Betty's visit, though she supposed that was not surprising. Sewell had had more impact on her life than any other man but it wasn't entirely to do with him.

On the basis of what Betty had told her, Nadine had felt free to let Sewell dominate her sexual imagination again but that was not the reason she had experienced such a strong desire for sex last night with Paul. That, she knew, was to do with re-establishing her sexual orientation. The experience with Betty had shocked her. She had no idea she could get such pleasure with a woman. If she had not gone through the rites of passage Sewell had initiated, she would have had to say honestly that no man had ever given her the feelings Betty had stirred in her. She would have begun to wonder if the reason for the mediocre experiences she had had with men was because she was performing with the wrong sex. Fortunately she had been able to comfort herself with the memory of what had happened with Sewell the first time, before Betty had come on the scene.

But she had needed more tangible proof and Paul had been the vehicle, the nearest man to hand. But Paul had himself proved to be more than just a convenient phallic substitute for Sewell.

Paul was an enigma. Both her sexual experiences with him had been thoroughly exciting and exciting in a totally different way from her encounters with Sewell. Her experiences with Sewell had been on the level of animal lust, of all-embracing, overwhelming sexual need. With Paul it had been more objective, more intellectual, like a sexual game to be played by a set of rules she did not yet understand. Paul's sexuality was a dark secret that needed to be unlocked, like the second door in his bedroom. She would like to have explored further but the funny thing was that Sewell had given her both the capability to unlock Paul's secrets and taken it away. Sewell had created her newfound interest in sex, making it possible for her to be aroused by the spectacle of what she had seen at the club in Paris and what she had done with Paul. But, at the same time, if there was a chance of being with Sewell, of having him on his own, of exploring her sexuality with him, Paul's secrets would remain undiscovered. Then the locked door – literally and metaphorically – would remain unopened.

As for the experience with Betty, Nadine had put

her own spin on that set of events. She had enjoyed having sex with a woman. But it all came back to Sewell. Sewell was enough for her, Sewell was what she wanted. Sewell had opened her up, had freed her of bourgeois sexual morality, had allowed her to appreciate the beauties of another woman's body. But, despite the fact she had slept with Betty, she knew if she was with Sewell, it would not be an experience she would yearn to repeat.

By the same token, she didn't want to share Sewell. That was the point. She was going to make it very clear to him that that was where she drew the line. Was that cutting off her nose to spite her face? She didn't think so. She loved the fact that she could now get untold pleasure from her own body but, in the end, she also had a mind and sharing Sewell's bed with another woman was not something she wanted to do again. Of that much she was sure.

Careful planning was required. The dinner: something that could be cooked in advance and needed no time in the kitchen. Her make-up: tarty and obvious. Her lingerie: stockings, of course, since he'd made so much fuss about them – sheer black stockings held taut by a thin satin suspender belt. No bra, no panties. Her perfume: a musky aroma that she hadn't worn before. Her dress: a black silk shift that left her shoulders and arms bare and swayed as she moved, its skirt just long enough to hide the welts of the stockings.

The irony was that, just as she'd left the office, the Brandling Corporation had called. It was official.

She'd got their account. The account that she'd hired Sewell for in the first place and which had started her adventure – which is how she'd come to think of everything that had happened to her – had come through on the night another major decision in her life was to be made.

More planning. What was she going to say? She knew she must not mention Betty's visit. She was going to say she had been foolish – or should she use the word bourgeois? – in her immediate reactions and that on reflection he had made such an impact on her life – that was true in spades – she would like to explore their relationship further. But she could not do that while he was living with another woman. That would give him the opportunity to tell her that she was all the woman he wanted, assuming what Betty had told her was correct.

She expected him to be late but she had everything ready by eight. To her surprise, it was only a couple of minutes past when the door bell rang.

Nadine adjusted her hair in the hall mirror and walked calmly to the door, resisting the temptation to run, telling herself, once again, not to behave like a love-sick teenager and reminding herself of the carefully reasoned arguments she had prepared. As she reached for the latch she saw that her hand was trembling.

'Hi,' she said brightly.

'Hi.' Sewell stood in the doorway. He was wearing brown corduroy trousers and a light tan shirt. He was smiling, grinning almost, his good humour radiating from his face like heat from the sun.

211

Nadine stared at him, every thought in her head wiped away, every line she had carefully prepared suddenly gone.

'Can I come in?' he asked after a silence of some seconds.

'Oh . . . yes, come in please,' she said flushed and flustered.

'For you,' he said offering her a large bunch of red roses.

'They're lovely,' she said as she stood aside to let him in. The hall was narrow and he brushed her as he passed by.

'And so are you,' he said. 'You look wonderful.'

As Nadine closed the front door he put out his hand to touch her shoulder, perhaps expecting her to pull away. But she didn't. His hand was warm. She felt as though he had touched her with a live electric wire. He moved his hand to stroke her neck.

'Oh Sewell . . .' She dropped the flowers onto the hall table.

There was nothing else she could say. She found herself in his arms, her lips pressed against his, their tongues vying for possession of each other's mouth, their bodies locked together. She felt his erection growing rapidly against her belly and her own excitement moistening her sex.

It was as though everything that had happened since she last saw him had simply dissolved. She couldn't remember anything but how good it felt to be in his arms. She couldn't remember a single thing she had planned to say to him. Her passion had washed it all away like sand castles in the flowing tide.

Not another word was spoken. Sewell picked her up and carried her like a baby up the stairs. Her bedroom door was open and he laid her on the bed and then fell on top of her, kissing her mouth, her cheeks, her neck, his hands all over her, moulding themselves to her breasts, stroking her legs, discovering her stockings and the nakedness of her sex. She scrambled to undo his shirt, fought with the belt of his trousers and the zip of his flies. They reached their objective at the same moment, his finger prying between her labia as her hand pulled his erection from his trousers.

They struggled with their clothes, reluctant to break the contact with each other. Her dress and his shirt were disposed of easily but it was impossible to wrest his trousers off. He pulled away from her and stood up, kicking his shoes off and stripping down his pants and trousers together. He wasn't wearing socks.

The uncoupling changed the mood. Naked, Sewell stood looking down at Nadine's body, registering the black stockings and the long thin fingers of satin suspenders, and what they meant — that she had been expecting to go to bed with him. He looked at her firm round breasts riding high on her chest despite the fact she was lying down and the delta of her pubic hair framing her labia, the vertical mouth of her sex. Above the welts of the stockings, her thighs seemed, by contrast, incredibly soft and creamy, infinitely touchable.

She, in turn, looked from the limpid pools of his dark brown eyes down to the hardness and strength of the cock that stuck out from his belly. She wanted to suck it, handle it, and have it inside her all at the same time.

She stretched out her hand until her fingers could touch his thigh. She drew one fingernail, newly varnished and manicured, down through the mat of black hairs, hard enough to make a track in his flesh, hard enough to hurt. She ran the same finger up to the top of the other leg then grabbed his cock in her fist, squeezing it hard like the handle of a lever. The glans, which stuck out from the top of her fingers, swelled. It was the last thing she could remember doing consciously.

His big powerful body smothered her and his cock was embedded inside her almost before she realised it. He thrust into her, his need for her so overwhelming and so evident that she was swamped emotionally as well as physically.

They were fused together. Nadine had never felt anything like this before. His cock was hard and strong and it filled her completely. She could think of nothing else but its power and its heat and its strength. It took her over. In seconds, she felt her body react, the engine of her orgasm beginning to turn, accelerating rapidly, the stimulation greater than anything she had ever felt, even with Sewell. How many times had she imagined him inside her? But the reality was better than the fantasy.

She clung to him, her arms wrapped around the hardness of his body just as her sex was wrapped around the hardness of his phallus. It was impossible to distinguish between their flesh. His whole body possessed her, owned her, was her.

Her orgasm exploded so quickly that in other circumstances it would have been embarrassing. But she didn't care. She didn't care about anything apart from being with him and having him inside her. She felt her body gush, a tide of her juices breaking over the head of his cock almost as though she had come like a man, soaking him and running out of her sex, so much she could feel wet trailing down her buttocks. She had never experienced such a thing before.

Sewell wasn't moving in her. He just remained still, pressing his cock up into her. She came again, this time the feeling centred in her clitoris, trapped between their pubic bones, crushed by the base of his cock. The waves of sensation spread through her until all her nerves were quivering with pleasure – her nipples, the tips of her fingers, right down to her toes. Most of all she came in her mind at the thrill of seeing Sewell again and feeling him. The desire, pent up for so long, released at last. She knew what he meant to her but she had tried, desperately, to ignore it.

'Sewell, Sewell . . .' Did she say it or was she only hearing it in her mind?

That was only the beginning. She couldn't count how many times he took her to the brink of orgasm then pitched her over it. Different things set her off, lighting the blue touch paper and detonating the explosions. She came as he touched his lips against her neck. She came as she felt his cock pulse inside her. She came as he began thrusting into her. She came as he arched his body to sink his teeth into her nipple. She trembled and shook wildly, caring about nothing but her own satisfaction.

It was not just Sewell's hardness and strength that was making her come but his instincts. He knew how to draw the passion out of her. Just when she thought she could take no more Sewell seemed to sense it. Ceasing the relentless thrusting, he held her still as he knelt in front of her, his cock buried in her sex. He could see her labia closed tightly around the base of his shaft, his cock and her sex glistening with the copious juices his first assault had produced.

In this position she could see him looking at her, his hands holding her just below her knees. He had parted her legs, splaying them out to the side, and she saw his eyes roaming her body, her face, her breasts, the furrow of her labia. She raised her head and looked at his phallus plugged into her. She squeezed it with the muscles of her sex and saw it throb.

Instantly she felt her body tense again, her excitement sparked by the expression on Sewell's face, an expression of desire and lust – and other, more complicated emotions. Perhaps Betty had been right about his feelings for her.

As Nadine felt herself tossed on the sea of another stormy climax, she felt Sewell's cock throbbing rhythmically. She struggled to keep her eyes open so as to watch as his body was rocked

216

by pleasure and he gave into her at last. She savoured the moment as he pushed forward once more into the dark and secret cavern of her sex. The rhythms of his body did the rest. His cock spasmed, once, twice and then a third time and his semen jetted out of him and his whole body shuddered as his seed spattered inside her. She watched as every muscle in his body locked and his mouth set in a grimace of ecstasy.

Their bodies were hot and sweaty. Perspiration ran down between Nadine's breasts and dripped from Sewell's forehead. One of Nadine's stockings was laddered along the calf and her hair was dishevelled. They were both breathing heavily but this was only the beginning. The initial throes of passion had been satisfied but not the passion itself.

Sewell lowered her legs. His cock was softening slowly and he pulled it out of her, looking down at the wet sheet under her buttocks. He moved around to kneel at her shoulder. It was obvious what he wanted and Nadine wanted it too. Turning on her side she used her hand to feed his cock into her mouth, gobbling it up hungrily, tasting her own juices mixed with his.

As her tongue circled the rim of his glans and she cupped his balls in her hand she felt him growing. He turned her on her back again, swinging his thigh over her head so he was poised above her. He lowered his head between her thighs, down into the lake he had created, his tongue teasing out her engorged clitoris and shocking it with sensation as he pushed it back against her hard pubic bone. Caressing her like this had a startling effect on his erection, which now swelled to its former proportions in her mouth.

As he manipulated her clitoris, Nadine pulled away so she could get her lips under his shaft, down to his balls. She sucked each one in turn into her mouth, then she used her tongue on his thick tool, teasing it with her teeth, biting him lightly all the way up to his glans, then swallowing him again, swallowing as deeply as she could, until he was buried in her throat.

She would have loved him to come there, loved to feel his cock jerking and spasming and his hot, sticky semen jetting into her throat. The thought made her sex convulse against Sewell's mouth, exciting him further.

On and on it went, a roller-coaster of sex seemingly with no end. Sewell's artful tongue and probing fingers soon revived Nadine's sexual energy. In minutes she felt her body gathering its strength again under the new assault on her senses. The feeling of his hardness in her mouth, linked with the feelings he was generating in her clit, sent her spiralling into another orgasm.

On and on it went until they were joined again, she riding him this time, bucking and bouncing on his erection, feeling its hardness invading every inch of her sex. She knew he would come again. She would make him come again. There was no need for talk, no need to work anything out, it was all there in the compass of her bed. The statement had been made, their bodies led the way and their minds followed.

In truth, it didn't matter what she thought. Nothing mattered, no consequences or implications. All that mattered was this.

Chapter Eight

'Paul, I promise you, it's not that.'

A pianist was playing 'Unforgettable'. The bar was lavishly decorated in deep blues, with small circular tables and leather armchairs that were a little too small.

'It was a mistake.'

'Look, I'm a big girl. I didn't do anything with you I didn't want to do. You know it excited me.'

'Really?'

'Yes, really. I wanted it as much as you did. If this hadn't happened I would have liked to explore further. I know you have secrets. I find that exciting.'

'Do you?'

'Yes, Paul, what can I do to convince you?'

'There *is* another man then?'

'Paul, it was all my fault. If I had been more honest with myself I could have been more honest with you. But I wasn't. I just didn't want to admit that he had such a hold over me. And anyway, even if I had, I thought it was all over.'

'Do you think it will last?'

'If you want the truth, I haven't the slightest idea.'

'Tell me about him?'

'No.'

'Why not?'

'Because there's no point. You're just very

221

different that's all. If I'd met you before him things might have been different.' That was a lie, she knew, but she felt so guilty about Paul she would have said anything.

'Nadine, I . . .' He stopped himself. She could see him wrestling to form a thought. 'I felt there was something about you, something I responded to, that I'd never found before.'

'Not even in your wife?'

'Especially not in my ex-wife.' He emphasised the word 'ex'. 'I know it's a cliché but she just didn't understand. She didn't care about what I wanted.'

'Wanted?'

'Do you think sex is important in a relationship?'

'Very.' Nadine would not have answered so positively weeks before.

'I just felt you were prepared to be . . .' he searched for the right word '. . . open.'

'And she wasn't? Is that the reason you got divorced?'

'Oh yes. My ex was only prepared to have sex in the missionary position, once a fortnight.'

'Sounds very familiar.'

'Does it?'

'It's a very easy pattern to fall into.'

'I hope you know, if this doesn't work out I'll be waiting for you.'

'No, you won't. You'll have found some outrageously beautiful woman and be having a wild affair. I don't want you to wait, Paul.'

'I know. And I have no intention of sitting around on my own. I just have a feeling it's going to be very difficult to find someone as interesting as you.'

Nadine sipped the large gin and tonic she had ordered. Paul was looking at her earnestly but he seemed to be taking the news very well. She had been with Sewell constantly over the last week and, when Paul had failed to reach her at home, he had finally rung her office. After what they had done together she thought it was only fair to tell him face to face.

She had no regrets at telling him about Sewell but, though once she would never have dreamt it possible, as she looked at Paul now she felt a pulse of excitement. She could not forget the things they had done. Paul was an enigma, a well of sexual feelings that ran deep. After their last encounter, lying naked on his bed with a blindfold over her eyes, she had wondered what new games he would want her to play. She was still curious.

'Will you tell me something?' she said in a serious tone.

'Anything.'

She was being foolish. It was nothing to do with her now but curiosity got the better of her.

'What's behind the locked door in your bedroom?'

'Is there one?' he fenced.

'You know there is.'

'All my secrets.' He smiled, a glazed expression on his face.

'Secrets?'

'If you had come to my house again I had every intention of showing you,' he said.

'Is that a promise?'

'Certainly.'

'It sounds intriguing.'

'From what I know about you, Nadine, I think you're the only woman who would be genuinely excited by it.'

'It?'

'By my secrets.' He smiled, a little shyly, she thought.

It was a smile that said a great deal. He obviously felt that this meeting with Nadine was not the last.

'I must go,' she said, knowing her attitude to Paul had subtly changed. She had thought she could dismiss him from her life with barely a thought and not an ounce of regret. But instead she found herself thinking about the things they had done together. She found herself wondering what lay behind the locked door in his bedroom and wanting to explore it. That did not mean, of course, she had any intention of doing so.

'You've got my number,' he said.

'This really is goodbye, Paul.'

'I know that. It's very nice of you to come for a drink. I appreciate it.'

'You gave me a very good time.'

She shook his hand, smiled wanly and walked out of the bar, conscious that his eyes were following her the whole way. Was that the last time she would see Paul? He had reacted differently from how she had imagined. He had been annoyed, but not indignant and it was perfectly clear to Nadine that she could walk back into his life at the drop of a hat. The question was whether she ever would. And that, of course, like everything that had happened to her since he'd first walked into her office, was up to Sewell.

'A little to the left,' he instructed. 'Perfect. Just open your legs a little more.'

Her legs were clad in sheer black hold-up stockings. He had brought the shoes. Their heels were so high she was almost standing on tip-toe. She would never have been able to wear them for normal use and could only manage to totter around but they shaped the muscles of her legs and increased the pout of her buttocks.

The shutter of the camera clicked and the tiny electric motor whirred as it wound the film on to the next exposure.

'Don't do anything. Just look into the lens.'

She was standing in his cream bedroom, her legs slightly apart, her breasts and sex quite naked.

'Cup your breasts in your hands.'

She did as she was told.

'No, so I can see the nipples. Yes, that's better.'

Nadine moved her hands so they were under the meat of her breasts and the nipples were bare. She had never been photographed like this before, open and nearly naked. Sewell wanted to paint her in stockings. She had modelled endless colours and styles for him but none had met his artistic requirements until she'd tried on a pair of hold-ups with broad welts made entirely from black lace. He preferred that. The suspender belts detracted from her waist and the suspenders would ruin the image of her thighs. In the painting, that was, not in life. In real life he loved the suspenders, ran his fingers along them, played with them with his tongue and caressed them as he pumped his cock into her. But in painting, apparently, different standards applied.

Nadine had spent most of the last three weeks in this bedroom. She could not help feel a nascent sexual excitement. The lens of the camera, Sewell had told her to imagine, was a large black phallus, probing and investigating her body. It should excite her, he said, though the truth was it was Sewell himself, naked behind the lens, that made her body throb.

It was her excitement he wanted to capture, the ways her body reacted, the infinite ways it responded to stimulus, the ways he would capture on canvas. But he needed more than that of course.

After three reels of film he set the camera on a tripod and pointed it at the bed.

'What now?' she asked.

'Us.' He was attaching a long lead to the shutter release.

'Us?'

'Together.'

'Doing it?'

'Yes.'

Nadine felt a kick of pleasure. Why did that idea thrill her so much?

'I have to have a picture as you come. That's what I want to paint.'

Coming with Sewell was certainly not a problem. She could never have imagined how much pleasure it was possible to get from her body, how it could be made to deliver sensations that left her shattered and drained and yet wanting more. But Sewell knew. What Sewell had promised in the beginning, he had delivered. He knew her body better than she knew it herself; he knew what she needed.

'You're already hard,' she said as he finished arranging the camera.

'Of course I am.'

'I thought this was all in the name of art. Objective and dispassionate. You're just a dirty old man taking dirty pictures.'

'I'm not old. Anyway, what do you expect with your body? Do you have any idea what you look like?'

'No, but I will when you develop the pictures.'

With the cord of the shutter release in his hand, Sewell climbed onto the bed.

'Sit on me,' he said lying on his back across the bed. 'Make sure your face is pointing right into the lens.'

'Very romantic. You're sure these aren't going to be sold to some men's magazines. I don't want my clients seeing pictures of me next to their adverts.'

'What a good idea. I'd make a fortune. Don't lose the mood.'

'What mood?'

'You're supposed to be having an orgasm remember?'

'With you, Sewell, that's hardly a problem.'

She swung her thighs over his hips and felt the heat of his cock nudging up between her labia. His hands fell on the lacy welts of her stockings and caressed them and the creamy soft flesh above. He has positioned the camera perfectly. Nadine could see her own reflection in the lens.

'You're beautiful,' he said.

Slowly she allowed herself to sink onto his cock. However many times she had sex with him she didn't think she'd ever get over the sensation of it stabbing into her. He always felt so hard, as hard as a bone.

'Oh Sewell,' she breathed, the levity gone, as her body melted over him.

He reached up to roll one of her nipples between his fingers while he worked the shutter release with his other hand. She heard the camera click, recording the first markers on the well trodden path she had travelled so many times. The noise thrilled her, increasing the pulse of her body, propelling her along the track.

He bucked his hips and rode up into her, moving his hand down from her breast to his belly. He pushed his finger between her labia and found the nub of her clitoris. He wanted her to come quickly.

He was seeing what the camera was seeing, her face registering the tension in her body, her nipples as hard as pebbles, her legs parted, the lacy welts dividing the thigh in two.

'Do it,' he said.

'Yes.'

Nadine felt her body surge as her sex clung to his cock and his finger stroked her clitoris from side to side. She sunk down on him lower, spreading her thighs apart, grinding herself down on him, acutely aware of the lens of the camera.

Click. Click. Click.

'I'm coming,' she said as if he didn't know, as if every part of her wasn't telling him, as if he couldn't feel the convulsions of her sex. She was coming on the tiny movement of his finger and the rock solid phallus that filled her. She was coming over him and for him, but there was an extra dimension. She was coming for the camera. She wanted it to see what he did to her, wanted every detail recorded so he could paint her as he had painted Betty and the other women. Paint the ecstasy she experienced and capture what they had together, a moment of time preserved forever.

The camera was forgotten. Sewell's needs asserted themselves. He dropped the shutter release, sat up, and took Nadine by the shoulders, pushing her roughly over to one side and arranging her so she was on all fours. Then he plunged his cock into her again, kneeling behind her and pummelling into her, watching his cock disappear into her sex and reappear newly anointed with her juices. He held her hips tightly, pulling her back onto him and driving into the depths of her.

He felt her shuddering too, another orgasm sweeping over her on the back of his passion.

He stroked into her hard then pulled his cock all the way out, catching it with his hand and holding it firm, pushing it up into the small puckered opening of her anus. It was wet from the juices that had run down from her sex when she was on top of him. Without waiting for her to protest, he pushed against the unyielding ring of muscles.

'No, Sewell,' she begged.

'Nadine.'

'I can't.'

'Please.'

She allowed him to push again but it was too late. Her muscles were locked and tight and however she tried she could not release them. He had tried to take her this way several times and she wanted to give him what she had never given any man. But she could not. Her body refused to co-operate. He had managed to get an inch or two inside but the shock of pain, a pain that had given her not the slightest hint of pleasure, had rocked through her and locked her shut as surely as if she had turned a key.

She promised him she would try. She wanted it. She wanted to feel it and even believed she would like it after she had managed to relax. But not yet. It was just too soon.

'Nadine,' he begged, knowing it was no good.

He pulled his cock up onto the top of her buttocks. It glistened under the lights. He picked up the cord for the shutter release and for no particular reason allowed the lens to photograph the moment.

'I'm sorry . . .' Nadine mumbled.

She reached down between her legs, caught the sack of his balls in her hand and pulled them tight. She felt his cock throb in the cleft of her buttocks. His hand circled it and he began to pump it in his fist.

'Yes,' she encouraged. 'Let me feel it.'

He pumped harder and harder, punishing himself,

almost hurting himself until his cock was full of semen. With three more strokes it jerked reflexively and spat out a string of hot white spunk all over the curves of her buttocks and over her long slender back.

Betty had moved out. In fact she had always kept her own flat, suspecting Sewell would tire of her in time, so only her clothes had gone. Sewell had promised Nadine that he would not want to share his life with anyone else but her and so far had appeared devoted to her. But Nadine had not moved in. She kept some clothes in the wardrobe and some underwear in one of the drawers in the bedroom, but that was all. So far. If they were going to be together they would have to get another house. But house-hunting was not a priority at the moment. Nadine was quite content to wait and see.

Besides, the more she lived with Sewell and the happier they were together, the more Nadine became convinced that it would not last. She hoped she was wrong. She hoped he would be able to change but she feared the attraction of the sort of freedom he had been allowed before would inevitably reassert itself. Strangely though, the thought did not upset her as much as she might have imagined. What Sewell had brought to her life, a vividness and energy and, most of all, a realisation that sex could be a potent source of almost unlimited pleasure, could not be taken away. If Sewell was as good as his word, she would, eventually, suggest regularising the situation. In the meantime, she was happy to lead a nomadic life, calling in at her house to pick up what she needed on the way to spend the night with him.

She found herself thinking about Paul. The way they had parted, and the things that he had said, had left an impression on her she could not forget. She wondered what lay behind the locked door in his bedroom and had wild flights of fancy that often left her feeling excited. It was a curious thought that if she had not first met Sewell she would probably never have been aware that at the centre of Paul's sex life was an enigma. Sewell had increased her threshold of sexual awareness to such an extent that she would never be able to go back to a relationship that contained the sexual fudges and compromises that had characterised her sexual encounters before. If she ever saw Paul again, the door would have to be unlocked.

But, of course, she could not hedge her bets. It had been necessary to be honest with Paul. The fact he had asked to be the first person she called should things not work out with Sewell was none of her doing.

But, it so happened, he was.

She had got home late. The Brandling Corporation were demanding clients and thought nothing of calling a meeting at five that would frequently go on till nine. But the amount of money they spent meant they could get away with it. No one was going to turn around to the Brandlings and tell them they should keep more sociable hours.

It was getting cold now, the first chill of autumn succeeding what had been one of the most pleasant summers for years. Nadine had stopped off at her house to get a coat for the morning. She had done nothing more than run in and out, however, keen to see Sewell. She hoped he had not yet eaten so they could go out to dinner and let a bottle of red wine wash away the tensions of the day.

She let herself into Sewell's house and saw a large sheet of paper had been fastened to the back of the door: GONE TO GALLERY. She knew what it meant. Since she had been involved with Sewell she had tried to persuade him to show his work. She had even made enquiries with a friend of Barbara's who wrote an art column for a Sunday paper and he had introduced Sewell to a gallery. Over the past two months Sewell had regularly taken paintings to the gallery and worked with them to plan the first major exhibition of his work. Discussions as to which paintings were to be included were taking ever more time.

The painting of Nadine was in progress and whenever she found herself alone in the house she was tempted to mount the bare wooden stairs to the attic and peak at it – though Sewell had expressly forbidden her to see it. Tonight was no exception. She got as far as the attic door but in the end turned towards the bedroom instead.

She undressed and showered, ate some bread and cheese and drank red wine. Then she climbed the stairs again and enjoyed snuggling down into Sewell's bed, the bed where it had all begun and where ever since, her sensual education had continued. She had a good book and was quite content with the prospect of reading until Sewell got home. Then, she decided, she would seduce him. Her body pulsed at the thought. Perhaps a time would come when the thought of sex with him would not make her melt but it was a long way off.

The book lasted three pages. The central heating was on and the room was warm and she was so comfortable in the bed she decided to rest her eyes for a few minutes. She fell fast asleep.

'Stop it!'

The voice woke her. It was feminine and light and full of laughter. She heard footsteps on the stairs.

'I've never done anything like this.' The voice came from the landing.

'Is that significant?' Sewell replied in a half-whisper.

'I'm scared.'

'Come on, Jane, it's me you're talking to. You're excited. You know you are. Why pretend?'

'I'm not pretending. I'm excited but I'm scared too.'

'Come here . . .'

Nadine sat up. She calmly closed the book that lay open on the bed and put it on the bedside table. The bedroom door was open and she could hear them kissing.

Sewell walked in, a boyish grin on his face.

'You're awake,' he said.

'Evidently,' Nadine replied.

The girl stood behind him in the doorway. He put his arm around her and pulled her into the room.

She was blonde, very blonde, with long straight hair that seemed to radiate light. She was tall and slender. She was also naked. Her breasts were small and she had very narrow hips, like a boy, with a marked tan unblemished by bikini lines. Her blonde pubic hair was thick and curly, not triangular but shaped like a cigar lying flat on her belly. It looked as though the shape was a natural phenomenon.

'Hello,' Jane said nervously.

Sewell sat on the bed. He was naked too. Obviously they had both undressed downstairs.

'She's pretty, isn't she?' he said.

Of all the myriad emotions Nadine felt, there was one that dominated everything. As she looked at the blonde's naked body she felt a wave of desire – strong, throbbing desire that took her completely by surprise. She felt her nipples stiffen and her sex moisten.

'Very,' she heard herself saying. 'Where did you find her?'

'She works at the gallery.'

'His paintings are just great, aren't they?' Jane said. For the first time Nadine detected an Australian accent.

'Yes, they are. Perhaps he'll paint you.'

Nadine pulled the bedding back and got up though she had no idea why. Was she intending to walk out?

'He said you were beautiful,' the Australian said, looking at Nadine's body. 'I'm really into women,' she added, sitting down next to Sewell. The words made Nadine's heart pump faster.

'See,' he said as if that was a justification.

'See what?' Nadine said. She couldn't stop looking at the blonde.

'I thought it would make a change for you.' He was still grinning sheepishly.

'For me?' Nadine could not keep the anger out of her voice.

She had known this moment would come, though she had hoped it wouldn't, but her reaction to it was a surprise. Of course she felt that Sewell had betrayed all the promises he had made her but at the moment that seemed immaterial. In the foreground of her emotions was the same desire she had felt for Betty. All the feelings Betty had aroused in her were suddenly released again. She had taken a conscious decision to repress that episode but it appeared that, given the chance, her body had other ideas.

She looked at Sewell. His dark brown eyes were watching her. As long as she had known him there had always been an element of mystery in his eyes, as though he knew something about the world she could never hope to understand. Tonight, for the first time, his mystery seemed to have disappeared. What she saw in his eyes instead was a challenge, a challenge to confront her own feelings. Was that just her imagination? His life, his values, his standards were not hers but if she left now it would seem like she was running away.

As if to prove she had nothing to fear, she walked up to the blonde and stood directly in front of her. She deliberately stroked the girl's nipple with the back of her hand.

'Nice,' the girl said.

Nadine didn't go any further. She had proved she was not frightened of her own emotions or desires. She could walk out now, walk not run, if that is what she chose. Instead, she dipped her head and kissed the girl lightly on the cheek. She could walk away now. Instead she moved her lips onto the girl's large fleshy mouth and kissed her without using her tongue. She could walk away without the slightest difficulty. Instead she allowed her tongue to push into the girl's mouth.

Why should she leave? This was going to be the last time. The last time in this situation. She had coped with it before. It had been an experience she had regretted but not one she would ever forget. Why not again, for the last time?

She straightened up. Jane was looking at her like a puppy dog wondering who was to be its new master. She put her hand out and touched Nadine's left breast.

'Great breasts,' she said, tweaking one nipple. 'Are you going to love me?'

If she had said 'fuck' or 'suck' or 'screw' or any one of a hundred crude expressions Nadine might well have walked away. But she didn't. She had said precisely what Nadine wanted to hear and she could not resist. Her mind told her she should go, but her body had control. Her body wanted those unfamiliar feelings again, the softness of a woman's body against hers, of breast against breast, of belly against belly.

Gently she pushed the girl back, twisting her around so she lay flat along the bed. Sewell got to his feet. Nadine lay beside her, looking up at Sewell. She told him with her eyes that this was not for him but for her.

Almost immediately Jane rolled on top of her, kissing her on the mouth, pushing her tongue between her lips and pressing her body down until Nadine's breasts were crushed between them. Her thigh slid between Nadine's legs and pushed up against her sex. Nadine felt a surge of pleasure.

Pulling away slightly, the Australian snaked her hand down between their bellies and into Nadine's labia. As she pressed up firmly with her thigh she found Nadine's clitoris with her finger and began to work it up and down.

'Love this,' she whispered, relinquishing Nadine's mouth only to kiss her neck and her collar bone then nibble on both breasts. Nadine gasped as Jane sunk her teeth into her nipple.

Slowly she worked her mouth down Nadine's body, moving her thigh from between Nadine's legs and kneeling beside her. Her tongue teased Nadine's pubic hair as her finger continued to massage her clit. Then she took it away and quite suddenly replaced it with her mouth.

Her mouth was hot, soft and wet. She parted Nadine's legs with her hands then began to lick the whole delta of her sex, like licking an ice cream, using her hands under Nadine's buttocks to tilt her sex up so her tongue could reach from the puckered crater of Nadine's anus to the top of her labia. After seconds of this she plunged her tongue into Nadine's vagina, wriggling it around like a tiny cock. Then her mouth slid up to Nadine's clitoris, her tongue lapping with practised ease, pushing it back against the pubic bone, while her fingers insinuated into Nadine's wet sex, two at first, then three, long thin fingers that excavated deeply.

Nadine's body tensed. She felt the motor of orgasm start instantly. The girl's fingers probed up inside her and caressed the silky wet vagina as Nadine wriggled down on them. She couldn't tell whether it was from this or from the hot tongue on her clitoris that she derived most pleasure. It was a race to see which part of her could turn the spiral of orgasm faster. Nadine's body arched off the bed and she gasped as the pressure became greater and then, like steam venting from an escape valve, her body exploded in orgasm, a sharp-focused almost painful pleasure that left Nadine weak.

Briefly the Australian lifted her head, a glint of triumph in her eye, then went back to work, her tongue softer now and more soothing, as were her fingers. Soon the journey of orgasm would begin again.

Nadine had been taken completely by surprise. She had been plunged very subjectively into a tide of feeling that had engulfed her. It was almost as if she were dealing with her confused emotions by channelling them in one direction, the sight of the slim girl and the feeling of what she had done to her pushing everything else aside.

She sat up and supported herself on her elbows to watch the blonde's long hair sweeping her thighs, her head moved from side to side. Sewell was watching the girl too, standing by the side of the bed. Nadine's feelings towards him were unfathomable. Her anger had been overcome by lust. Perhaps it *was* all right, perhaps it didn't matter once in a while. Sewell didn't seem to see it as a betrayal of their relationship and, at least, his infidelity was not a secret and involved her. Had her initial anger been the product of her own insecurities? Had the doubts about her experiences with Betty suddenly resurfaced?

Maybe it didn't have to be the last time after all. She could cope with this. In fact, judging from what she was feeling, she would welcome it. Once in a while.

Sewell looked into her eyes. She remembered the first time she had seen him and the impact he had had on her. He was looking at her with such tenderness and with a plea for understanding that it was impossible for her to resist. She wanted to please him because he had given her so much, had showed her how to use her body and had been responsible for waking her from what she now thought of as a long, tiresome sleep. Her emotions took another sharp turn as anger turned to gratitude.

Nadine pulled the blonde by the shoulders.

'Both of us,' she said.

No other explanation was necessary. Nadine lay back again and opened her legs. The Australian swung her thigh over Nadine's waist, to sit astride her, then slid backwards until her sex was over Nadine's face and she could dip her mouth to Nadine's labia again.

As Nadine extended her tongue into the thick bush

of hair that covered Jane's sex, she wrapped her hands around the girl's thighs and used the fingers of one hand to nudge into the gate of her sex. As her mouth latched onto Jane's nether lips and her tongue probed to find the promontory of her clitoris, she felt Jane do the same to her.

Nadine loved this feeling, the circle of passion, the completeness of it, the feeling that only two women can have. What she did to the blonde, what she made the blonde feel, she felt too. It could never be like this with a man, she could never know what a man was feeling but she knew exactly what the blonde felt because she was feeling it herself. Now she could feel the first stirrings of orgasm in Jane's body, like a string of an instrument being plucked, and then the quickening tempo as sensations surged through her, her own body experiencing exactly the same reactions. She thrilled at the feeling of the blonde's hard nipples pressing into her belly and the soft smooth flesh that smothered her, and knew the blonde would feel the same.

Together, in a private communion, sealed from the world, they could build their own edifice of passion as quickly or as slowly as they liked. In fact it was very rapid. Nadine felt her pulse racing, propelling her forward, the world narrowing, as it always did, into the tiny compass of their two bodies. As she felt herself lurch into orgasm, the blonde came too, the two of them coming together, trembling and helpless together, wild and wanton together and, finally, drained and relaxed together as the tide of feeling ebbed away.

As Nadine opened her eyes she saw the Australian's tight boyish buttocks. She looked for Sewell. He was standing by the bedside table. He had taken something from the drawer on his side of the bed. It was a jar of cold cream, a blue jar which Nadine had never seen before, or never noticed at least. He smeared the cream on his cock. For a second Nadine had no idea what he was doing, distracted by the aftermath of sex that still played in her senses. Then she knew. The penny dropped.

'You never let me,' he said as he saw the expression on Nadine's face change.

And *she* would. Jane would. He was kneeling behind her, his hands on her small neat buttocks, parting them, pushing his phallus forward between them. His cock was right above Nadine's face, and she could actually see it pressing into the little round fistula of her anus, as Jane wriggled against it.

This was not the first time, they had done this before. This was not some casual girl he had brought home on a whim. Late nights at the gallery had provided an ideal excuse.

'No,' Nadine said squirming out from under the Australian's body.

Sewell took no notice. He held the blonde firmly by the hips and pushed forward. The blonde gasped, then squirmed appreciatively, clearly enjoying the experience.

For a moment Nadine stood looking at Sewell and he looked back at her. But he was not seeing her. Like a man on drugs his eyes were glazed. He wanted only what was laid out in front of him, there were no time for anything else.

'You bastard,' Nadine said quietly but Sewell made no reply, only pushing deeper, making the blonde squeal with delight.

'Love it,' she breathed.

Calmly Nadine found her dress and a pair of shoes. Downstairs she took her handbag and the raincoat that hung from the hall stand. She walked to the front door.

'God, God,' the blonde screamed, her voice echoing through the house.

Outside it was raining, cold hard rain coming down in straight lines. Even before she had reached her car Nadine's hair was soaked. But no tears joined the water running down her cheeks.

'It was a wonderful dinner.'

'Thank you.'

'Where did you learn to cook?'

'I just picked it up.'

'Well, you're very good.'

'Let's go and sit in the living room and I'll make some coffee.'

'I don't want coffee.' Nadine said.

'Brandy? Dessert wine?'

'Dessert wine.'

Nadine got up and walked through to the living room. She settled herself in one of the large sofas as Paul went into the kitchen. He returned with a silver tray on which was an open bottle of Chateau Yquem and two crystal glasses. He poured the golden wine and handed her a glass, sitting opposite her in an armchair.

'Cheers,' he said. 'Thanks for coming.'

'Thanks for inviting me. I'm still not sure I should have rung you.'

'Why not? I told you it would be all right.'

'What people say and mean are two different things.'

'Not in this case. We were friends.'

'No, Paul, we were lovers, that's entirely different.'

'Nadine, I told you, I didn't wait around. But no one else . . . how shall I put it? You're a very difficult act to follow. You are very beautiful.'

'Thank you.'

Nadine didn't feel beautiful. For the two weeks since she had left Sewell, she had felt wretched. She had been more confused and depressed than she had ever been in her whole life. She missed Sewell dreadfully and was missing having sex with him. He had changed her life and the change appeared to be permanent. Her sex life had no intention of being sidelined again. The temptation to go back to Sewell had been almost overwhelming.

She had resisted. During the encounter with the Australian blonde, she had decided that the occasional fling, open and above board, was not something she should mind, especially as she got as much pleasure out of it as Sewell did. She certainly wouldn't tolerate it being once a week but if Sewell occasionally brought home a waif or stray, she would enjoy the secret pleasure and not let it get in the way of their relationship.

But far from being open and honest, Sewell had lied to her. Like other men, other mere mortals, he had been having an affair behind her back and she resented it. She resented it all the more because, not only had she been seduced into making love to the girl, during their time together she had tried hard to give Sewell the one thing she had never done with any man. Her efforts had clearly not been appreciated.

She had also resisted the temptation to do what she had done after her first disappointment with Sewell, as much as she needed a man. She had resisted calling Paul for ten whole days.

When she had finally summoned the nerve to do it, she was put out to discover he was in America. But he had called her from Seattle. The dinner had been arranged and he had left her in no doubt that he was extremely pleased to hear from her again. She in turn had been extremely pleased to hear his voice.

She sipped the chilled wine and looked at him. He was wearing a white shirt and dark blue slacks with Gucci pumps. His eyes had barely left her all evening.

'Paul?' she said steadily.

'Yes.'

She hadn't been at all sure when she arrived at the house how she would feel about him. She had told him she just wanted to talk. But now she knew how she felt. Exactly how she felt.

'Would you take me upstairs?' She could have said that she wanted him to take her to bed, but that was not precise enough. She had spent some time thinking of Paul while she was with Sewell and, in the last two weeks, Paul had become part of her fantasies – the masturbation rites she had needed so badly to keep the dull ache of need at bay.

'Upstairs?' he said.

'You remember what we said?'

'I remember it very well.'

'Good.'

'And that's what you want?'

'Yes.'

She stood up and walked the two strides to his chair, standing in front of him so her legs touched his knees.

'I want to get to know you, Paul. Everything.'

'I thought . . .'

'What?'

'I thought I'd never see you again.'

'Well, here I am. Are you going to take me upstairs now?'

Paul got to his feet. He kissed Nadine gently on the lips then walked to a large Victorian partner's desk that was tucked in the far corner of the room. He opened a drawer and extracted a key on a silver chain.

He took her hand and led her up to the bedroom. The key fitted into the middle door of the three.

'There's something I have to do first,' he said.

'What's that?'

He produced a black silk blindfold from the pocket of his trousers. It was the same one he had used on her before.

'You were expecting this?' she said.

'Not expecting. I thought I should be prepared.'

She smiled, her mouth dry, her pulse racing. Her nipples were so hard they felt cold. Her sex was moist.

'Blindfold me, Paul,' she said, the words making her body shiver slightly.

She thought of Sewell, not because she wished she had been with him, but because he had started it all, had launched her on a voyage of discovery during which she had already visited uncharted waters. But the voyage, she now realised with growing excitement, had only just begun.

Cremorne Gardens

Anonymous

An erotic romp from the libidinous age of the Victorians

UPSTAIRS, DOWNSTAIRS . . .
IN MY LADY'S CHAMBER

Cast into confusion by the wholesale defection of their domestic staff, the nubile daughters of Sir Paul Arkley are forced to throw themselves on the mercy of the handsome young gardener Bob Goggin. And Bob, in turn, is only too happy to throw himself on the luscious and oh-so-grateful form of the delicious Penny.

Meanwhile, in the Mayfair mansion of Count Gewirtz of Galicia, the former Arkley employees prepare a feast intended to further the Count's erotic education of the voluptuous singer Vaźelina Volpe – and destined to degenerate into the kind of wild and secret orgy for which the denizens of Cremorne Gardens are justly famous . . .

Here are forbidden extracts drawn from the notorious chronicles of the Cremorne – a society of hedonists and debauchees, united in their common aim to glorify the pleasures of the flesh!

FICTION / EROTICA 0 7472 3433 7

Bonjour Amour

EROTIC DREAMS OF PARIS IN THE 1950S

Marie-Claire Villefranche

Odette Charron is twenty-three years old
with enchanting green eyes, few
inhibitions and a determination to make it
as a big-time fashion model. At present
she is distinctly small-time. So a meeting
with important fashion-illustrator Laurent
Breville represents an opportunity not to
be missed.

Unfortunately, Laurent has a fiancée to
whom he is tediously faithful. But Odette
has the kind of face and figure which can
chase such mundane commitments from
his mind. For her, Laurent is the first step
on the ladder of success and she intends to
walk all over him. What's more, he's
going to love it . . .

FICTION / EROTICA 0 7472 4803 6